'Take me home!' she muttered through gritted teeth. 'I've had enough. You don't have to keep this up. You've got me here now and I'll stay, regardless of the means you thought you had to employ to bring me here. For your information, they weren't necessary—in fact they had the opposite effect. You think you're so darned attractive that I just couldn't wait to get out here to you, but you're wrong, Alastair Drummond. I came here to work. So you can go happily back to your nice little romance or whatever you've got with Rowena MacMillan and leave me alone. I'm not here to play games.'

He stood and looked at her for an interminable moment, his eyes dark and unfathomable.

'Is that what you think?' His voice was tinged with anger. 'That I made love to you just to get you to come to Australia?'

'I don't know what your motives were in making love to me,' Claire snapped. 'All I'm saying is that I don't want it. Leave me alone!'

Marion Lennox has had a variety of careers—medical receptionist, computer programmer and teacher. Married, with two young children, she now lives in rural Victoria, Australia. Her wish for an occupation which would allow her to remain at home with her children, her dog and the budgie led her to attempt writing a novel.

Previous Title

DARE TO LOVE AGAIN

CRUEL COUNTRY

F.m.s

BY

MARION LENNOX

MILLS & BOON LIMITED
ETON HOUSE   18–24 PARADISE ROAD
RICHMOND   SURREY   TW9 1SR

First published in Great Britain 1990 by Mills & Boon Limited

© Marion Lennox 1990

Australian copyright 1990 Philippine copyright 1990 This edition 1990

ISBN 0 263 76886 4

Set in 10 on 12 pt Linotron Times 03-9007-50005 Typeset in Great Britain by Centracet, Cambridge Made and printed in Great Britain

CHAPTER ONE

DR CLAIRE BANNON retreated to the light of a shop window, checked her list and admitted she was trying to do too much. She had only allowed three hours tonight for Christmas shopping. Tomorrow was Christmas Eve and she was on duty. She glanced at her watch. An hour to go and she wasn't halfway through her list.

She should have shopped last Saturday on her rostered day off, but Casualty was frantic, so she had worked instead. That was the problem, Claire thought dejectedly. She could never object to the demands of work. She felt guilty if she did.

Guilt. It had been with her for ten years now, since she was seventeen. A stupid escapade by a couple of silly kids and she had to pay for the rest of her life. She eased the weight off her right leg. The limp was almost imperceptible now, but her leg still ached.

Claire closed her eyes and let the tiredness wash over her. One more day and then three blessed days off. The farm would be filling to bursting-point as her family gathered for Christmas. She had worked for the last three Christmases, but this year had promised to go home.

She couldn't go home without gifts. Resolutely she opened her eyes and launched her slight frame back into the throng of shoppers. As she reached the entrance to the store a high-pitched scream and squeal of brakes split the night.

Claire spun around towards the road. One of the scores of 'Santa's spreading sweets and Christmas cheer among the shoppers had attracted a little boy from the other side of the street. He had darted away from his mother's grasp, right into the path of the busy traffic. Before Claire's horrified gaze his body was caught and flung on to the bonnet of a large Rover. The car came to a sliding, skidding halt, with the child toppling like a broken doll on to the icy roadway.

The crowd surged forward. Claire's view was blocked. She dropped her shopping and pushed her way urgently through the crowd.

Pushing through a crowd was easier said than done, especially when one was five feet two, slightly built and lame. Claire had never regretted her lack of height more. Finally she raised her voice, pushing at the same time.

'Let me through, please—I'm a doctor.'

The crowd parted reluctantly, eyeing her with suspicion. Claire didn't look like a doctor. With her jeans, duffel coat and dark hair tied back in a pony-tail, she was more likely to be taken for someone's kid sister. Nevertheless, her voice belied her appearance as she invested it with all the authority she could muster.

The small group clustered over the child was harder to shift. The mother was there, crouched in the roadway sobbing hysterically. Two more children clutched her coat in bewilderment. Above them was the driver of the car.

He was in his thirties, Claire guessed, deeply tanned with a shock of fair hair and beard. His face reflected all the dismay of a driver caught in a nightmare situation. As Claire reached the group he seemed to collect himself and bent towards the limp body. She was there before him. As she gently edged the mother aside, the driver caught Claire by the arm, pulling her up. His voice was broad Australian.

'What the hell do you think you're doing? Leave him be. If you want to be any use, go and call an ambulance.'

Claire pulled herself up to her full height, aware that he towered over her.

'I'm a doctor. Let me see him, please. You've done enough damage already.' She was aware as she said it that her comment was unfair, but she wasn't in the mood to be tactful. She glared up at him and was aware of deeply set green eyes filled with anger. Their gaze held, alight with tension. For a moment she was mesmerised, locked into a conflict she didn't understand. In confusion, she tempered her voice. 'I suggest you move these people back.' From every side the crowd was moving closer.

'You? A doctor?' His voice was a mixture of derision and fury.

Claire didn't bother to reply. She stooped over the little boy and started work. For a moment the man above her hesitated as if he was considering forcibly hurling her from the scene. Somehow her professionalism must have penetrated, for finally he turned towards the crowd.

The Australian accent became less noticeable as he issued orders. Miraculously the pressing mill of people responded and Calire was left with some space. Her hands moved gently over the little boy, and she started making soft, reassuring noises as she realised he was still conscious.

The mother edged forward, and Claire's voice included her. For those moments they might have been alone in a hospital ward as Claire ignored the hubbub around them.

'Just keep quite still, little one. You've hurt your leg and it's very important that you don't move.' Her hands held him firmly. 'Soon we'll hear the ambulance. The ambulance men have a special stretcher, so we can move you to the hospital without hurting your leg even more. Have you ever been to hospital?'

The little boy's face looked up at hers, white with shock and pain. Claire stroked his face and smiled gently down at him.

'Look,' she motioned behind her, 'here's your mum. You've given her a big fright and made her cry, but she's OK now. She'll come in the ambulance with you to the hospital. The doctors there make sore legs better.' Behind her, the mother's sobs subsided as Claire's words took effect. The other two children, little girls aged perhaps two and three, whimpered and held her close.

Claire was conscious of the bearded driver above her and realised he was offering a thick car rug. She took it without looking up and wrapped the little boy as best she could without moving him.

They had only minutes to wait before a siren signalled the arrival of the ambulance. Claire looked up gratefully as two burly officers approached.

'Get out of it, Doc.' They grinned, recognising her. 'This is our work. Don't they give you enough to do in the wards? Surely you don't have to go out drumming up business?' Already they had summed up the situation and the stretcher was in place. Skilled hands moved the little boy on to the stretcher with minimum body movement. Claire made to disengage her hand from tiny fingers, but the fingers tightened and the mother's voice came as a thin whisper from behind.

'You'll come with us?'

Claire looked at the little family. The girl couldn't have been more than twenty-one or -two and was still in a state of shock. The two tots clinging to her coat were bedraggled and frightened; they were going to need all their mother's attention. The girl looked at her beseechingly. Beside Claire the fingers still clung and two little eyes looked trustingly into hers.

The ambulance officers moved the stretcher towards the ambulance and the fingers pulled her along. With a last despairing glance back at the lights of the shops, Claire allowed herself to be ushered on board.

The mother and little girls were handed up into the cabin and one of the officers came behind to climb in and close the doors. As he pulled the first door shut, the bearded Australian appeared. He addressed Claire directly.

'Is there anything I can do?'

Claire looked at him in frustration. If it weren't for this man she would still be Christmas shopping.

'You can find my shopping and finish my list,' she snapped at him, before the door closed in his face.

CHAPTER TWO

CHRISTMAS EVE for Claire was endless. Flu had swept through the staff, leaving the hospital desperately short-handed. As her personal price for having three days off over Christmas, Claire had worked for two weeks without a break, and each shift had stretched for hours on either side of her official time on and off. On Christmas Eve she was supposed to finish at six, but by the time there was a let-up in the patients needing to be seen before Christmas it was nearly eight. The last train home left at nine. Claire grimaced as she wished everyone Merry Christmas and left the casualty department. She glanced at her watch. She had promised to look in on Tim, the little boy she had cared for the night before, but it was going to run her perilously close to missing the train. She sighed. There was no choice. With hands deep in the pockets of her white coat she limped to the lift.

Tim was at the end of the ward, propped up on pillows. He showed little resemblance to the pathetic creature of the night before. Despite the huge white plaster encasing his leg he was back to being a boisterous, bouncy four-year-old.

His mother, father and two little sisters were with him, and Claire smiled at the sight of him holding court. His mother still looked drawn and tired, but otherwise the family seemed to have suffered no lasting ill effects. They greeted Claire with delight as she approached, all the children trying to talk at once.

'I'm going to have Christmas in hospital,' Tim announced proudly. 'And we're going to have ice-cream and lollies and balloons. And my leg's broken in three places. And Santa's coming!'

'It looks as if he's already been.' Claire grinned, gesturing towards the array of toys, books and puzzles littering the bed.

'It was the driver of the Rover from last night,' Tim's mother explained. 'He came in to see Tim half an hour ago and left all these—presents for Tim and for the girls.' She looked at up Claire, her eyes bright with grateful tears. 'I was so embarrassed. It wasn't as if it was his fault.' Backing into the security of her husband's encircling arm, she tried to frown at her son, but it didn't quite come off.

'Young scamp!' Her husband was more severe. 'I work in town and Jan brought the kids in to meet me,' he explained to Claire. 'Never again, though.' He held his young wife tightly and glared at his son. 'Not until you're twenty.'

Tim looked abashed for a whole five seconds, then whooped on another gift. Claire left them laughing, with a feeling of lightness around her. Perhaps Christmas really wasn't so bleak. She checked her watch and the feeling of lightness evaporated as if it had never been. Eight-twenty. It would take her a good thirty minutes to get to the station and she had to go back to her quarters for her bags and coat. The strict rule on never running in hospital corridors was abandoned forthwith. As fast as her stiff right leg allowed her, Dr Claire Bannon ran.

As she opened her bedroom door the phone rang. Grabbing her coat, she started pulling it on with one hand while she picked up the receiver in the other.

'Yes?'

'Dr Bannon, it's Ellen here on Reception. There's a Dr Drummond here to see you. Can you come over?'

Claire did a quick mental review. Dr Drummond? She didn't know a Dr Drummond. She shook her head.

'I can't—I'm catching a train in thirty minutes. It'll have to wait.' She hooked the receiver over her ear and pulled the other arm into a sleeve, then started to put the phone down.

'Dr Bannon?' Ellen's voice was urgent, and Claire hesitated. 'It's regarding last night's accident. He says he must see you.'

'But I'll miss my train!' Claire wailed.

'Apparently it's imperative that he sees you tonight. Sorry. I'll tell him you're on your way.' The phone went dead and Claire was left staring at a blank receiver.

She stood in the centre of the room and looked down at her closed suitcase. Imperative. Why, for heaven's sake? Was something wrong with Tim? She thought back to the bouncy little boy she had just left. Surely not. Had someone else been hurt? The driver? He had looked shaken, but certainly not hurt. Finally she looked at her watch. Thirty minutes until her train left. There was no way she could go back to the hospital and still get to the station on time. As it was, she was going to be very lucky to make it.

Finally a bleak acceptance washed over her. She hadn't bought half her gifts, she'd lost the other half, and now she was going to miss her train. The next train would be on Boxing Day, which would give her just one night at home before she had to return. She took off her coat and slowly made her way back through the covered walkway to the hospital reception, limping with tiredness. As she walked through the main doors, a tall, bearded figure rose from a chair to meet her—the driver of the Rover.

'You!' She spat the word with loathing, then looked around, confused. There was no one else in Reception.

He had started towards her, but stopped at the tone of her voice. Through her anger Claire was conscious of a sense of strength, of quiet assurance.

'I was told I was wanted by a doctor.' Her words were an accusation.

'I'm a doctor.' His voice was a soft drawl. He watched her, sensing her fury, waiting for her reaction.

It came, the pent-up tension and disappointment of the past twenty-four hours giving vent to icy anger.

'Damn you!'

His only response was eyebrows raised in polite enquiry, a look of faint amusement on his face. Luckily Claire had nothing in her hands—the urge to throw something was almost uncontrollable.

'Damn you!' she repeated through clenched teeth. 'Doctor or not, you can't possibly want me for any medical reason. First of all you destroy the only chance I've had in a fortnight to do any Christmas shopping for my family, and now you make me miss the last train home with your urgent messages. Damn you, damn you! I can't think of a thing you could need me urgently for, and there's nothing I need to say to you except if I never see you again it'll be too soon. I hope your Christmas pudding chokes you!'

To her fury she felt tears spilling down her cheeks as tiredness and the sense of loss of her lovely Christmas swept over her. She shook her head stupidly. 'This was the first time for three years that I could go home for Christmas. I hope you're satisfied!' She fought back a sob, turned and fled.

CHAPTER THREE

CLAIRE woke late on Christmas morning. By the time she'd rung her family on the previous evening and dissuaded them from undertaking the six-hour round trip to come and fetch her she was emotionally drained. She had spent a couple of sleepless hours asking herself deep questions such as why she hadn't studied typing instead of medicine. Finally she had given herself a good talking to, told herself she would be much more appreciated in the hospital than if she had gone home giftless, thrust away the infuriatingly persistent image of green eyes and an Australian drawl, and fallen asleep.

She lay cocooned in the warmth of her bedclothes, savouring the luxury of a sleep-in. If she couldn't go home for Christmas at least no one was going to pull her out of bed. The hospital staff thought she was in Yorkshire; let them go on thinking it for a while. Some time before lunch she would appear and give a hand in Casualty for the rest of the day. Casualty on Christmas afternoon was always horrendous, with injuries from new skateboards and roller-skates and reactions from over-indulgence in rich food.

She snuggled down and closed her eyes. The building was quiet; all the staff who weren't on duty had long since disappeared to their respective celebrations.

Sleep overcame her once again. She slept deeply, and woke only as insistent knocking echoed through the room.

For a moment she considered the idea of not answering the door. It was locked; whoever it was could just go away. She pulled the covers over her head and willed the knocking to stop. Suddenly her eyes sprang wide open. Perhaps her father or brother had ignored her refusal of their offers and had come for her anyway. With a bound she was out of bed, fumbling at the latch. She swung the door open and a huge, leafy aspidistra walked into the room.

Claire stood back in stunned silence. The plant passed her, crossed the room and deposited itself on the bed. As it came to rest a familiar figure emerged from underneath. The Australian.

For a moment she was too stunned to speak. Her visitor stood back, critically appraising the plant.

'Well? What do you think?'

'What on earth is it?' Claire was having difficulty making her voice work.

'A pot plant.' The same soft drawl.

Claire took a deep breath and fought to get her voice from squeak to normal.

'So what do I want with a pot plant?'

'It's not your pot plant,' he replied in the injured tone of one finding himself unappreciated. 'It's Auntie Lil's pot plant. Number eleven on the list, to be precise.' He groped in his pocket and produced a tattered piece of paper. With amazement Claire recognised her list, abandoned with her shopping at the scene of the accident.

'You haven't. . .' Her voice trailed away. She looked up into the deep green eyes and shook her head in bewilderment.

'That's right. Every item.' His tone was serious, but his eyes were alight with amusement. 'I had a spot of trouble with the twins, though. With everyone else you had a suggestion beside their name, but you just had a question mark beside them. It's a bit hard when you have to guess. Do you think these'll be OK?' His face creased into lines of anxiety and he gestured to the corridor. Sitting against the wall were two enormous teddy bears, one pink and one white. They regarded Claire with silly, lop-sided grins. She glared up at the big, fair man beside her, glared back at the teddy bers and tried desperately to control the urge to giggle. Her mouth twitched. She bit back the laughter, but it refused to be suppressed, bubbling out in a blessed release of tension.

The stranger's anxious face relaxed. He lounged back against the wall, grinning at her. Claire finally gained control again.

'The twins are sixteen years old—Laura and Michelle. They'll love them.'

'I'm glad.'

His grin had softened. The smile was gentle and somehow penetrating. Claire was caught in it, held.

She broke the moment, turning away with the beginning of a blush. She suddenly realised how little she had on—a flimsy lace négligé and bare feet peeping from the soft folds. The corridor was freezing. She backed self-consciously into her bedroom.

'Thank you. I suppose this is why you came to see me last night.'

'That's right.'

'And I screamed like a banshee at you.' Claire bit her lip. 'I'm so sorry.'

'Think nothing of it. I gather my visit was ill-timed, to say the least.'

She shook her head.

'It doesn't matter. I was running so late I probably would have missed the train anyway.' She hesitated, then continued resolutely, 'I'm sorry too for saying the accident was your fault. I know it wasn't.'

'That's OK too.' He was still leaning against the wall, his face reflecting gentle mockery.

'I. . .' Claire was right off balance. She struggled to maintain some semblance of dignity. 'I must owe you some money—I'll get my wallet.' She retreated further into the bedroom and turned to locate the wallet in a bedside drawer. As she turned back she gasped. He had followed her in and was standing three feet from her.

'Very cosy.' He gazed around appraisingly. 'Is this where you're spending Christmas this year?'

'I'll go over to the wards soon. There's plenty of work needs doing.'

'It'd be much better to be at home, though, wouldn't it?'

'Perhaps,' Claire agreed with him waspishly. This man had her badly rattled. 'But if I'm stuck here I may as well be useful.'

He nodded, his eyes not leaving hers.

'How much do I owe you?' Claire's voice sounded nervous even to her own ears.

'I don't take payment in cash.'

'But I must pay you. . .' Her voice trailed off. The gaze intensified and with a gasp she realised what he intended. Before she could as much as step back her face was caught between two strong hands and his mouth found hers.

It was a feather kiss, a light, questioning meeting of lips. The fair beard brushed the bare skin of her throat, sending a sudden shiver of response through her. With a gasp she jerked backwards, out of his grasp.

'What on earth are you doing?'

'I thought it was obvious.' The low voice sounded shaken and suddenly unsure. He stood watching her, the laughter faded from his eyes.

'You'd better go.'

'You can't blame me, you know.' The amusement edged back into his voice. 'If you entertain male visitors in your bedroom looking like that you've got to expect repercussions.'

'Looking like what?' she asked stupidly.

'Like that.' He seized her shoulders and spun her round to face the mirror.

Claire's eyes were huge and dark in her lovely face. Her curls were loose and tangled, matted from a restless night's sleep. They cascaded on to bare white shoulders, tendrils trailing down to the deep hollow between her firm round breasts. The nightgown was low-cut. Her breasts rose and fell in breathless rhythm. The lace was flimsy and revealing. Claire drew in her breath, pulled away and seized her dressing-gown from behind the door.

'Will you please leave?' She pulled her arms into the thick woollen sleeves.

'Not yet.'

'I can scream.'

'I'm sure you can.' He was laughing again. He held out his hand placatingly. 'It's probably time we met officially. I know who you are, Dr Claire Bannon— they told me when I enquired at the ambulance station. I was lucky enough to catch the crew who'd attended the accident before they came off duty last night. I'm Dr Alastair Drummond. I'm an Australian and, believe it or not, I'm respectable. I don't make a habit of kissing young women on second acquaintance—in fact I haven't done it for months. I'm here to ask you how you intend to get all your Christmas presents home to your family.'

Claire ignored the outstretched hand and glared at him.

'Are you really a doctor?'

'Yes.'

'A people doctor?'

The eyes creased in laughter. 'There's probably a more academic way of terming it, but yes, a people doctor. You haven't answered my question.'

Claire glared at him, totally confused. 'It's none of your business.'

'It is my business. I made you miss your train.' His voice was insistent. 'How, Dr Bannon?'

'I'm going home by train in the morning.'

The creases of laughter around his eyes deepened.

'With Frederick and Clarabel?' He gestured to the two bears in the corridor. 'And Auntie Lil's instant garden?'

Claire's glare intensified. She was way out of her depth and she knew it.

'I've a suggestion.' She opened her mouth to argue, but was forestalled by a finger pressed firmly over her lips. 'My car is at your disposal. Half your gifts are already in the luggage compartment. Frederick and Clarabel can keep the foliage company in the back seat and I'll drive you home——'

'But it's three hours' drive,' Claire broke in.

'Only three? Great.' He glanced at his watch. 'It's nine o'clock now. We'll make it in time for lunch.'

'For heaven's sake! You can't possibly be wanting to traipse into the wilds of Yorkshire on Christmas morning!'

'I was hoping for a free feed.'

'Oh, for heaven's sake——' Claire shook her head.

'Dr Bannon,' he interrupted. His eyes held an expression she couldn't fathom. 'Please allow me to take you home. It would be a pleasure.'

'The free meal?' she couldn't resist asking.

His eyes dropped. He sighed.

'I'm sorry—it was stupid of me. I'd forgotten your English class system. You probably don't want someone with my convict ancestry eating off my knife and generally lowering the tone of the place.' He pulled an imaginary cap off his head and held it humbly in front of him. 'I promise I don't expect more than a bowl of thin gruel in the servants' quarters. I'll behave very respectfully, call you ma'am all the way there, and as soon as I swallow my allotted gruel I'll come right back to town and get out of your life. Now what more could a girl ask from a deferential colonial?' He raised his head, eyed her wickedly and changed his tone.

'And furthermore, you have five minutes to get yourself respectable. I'll wait in the corridor. If you're not ready in the allotted time I'll break your door down, throw you over my shoulder and forcibly abduct you—nightie and all. And if you don't tell me where your parents live I'll take you back to my lodgings and give you the thin gruel.' He walked out.

Claire was left gazing wordlessly at the closed door. She felt as if all the breath had been pushed out of her. Her mind spun.

To go with him? The idea was absurd, dangerous

even. What did she know about him? The vision of her family intruded. She looked around at the four walls of her room. Stay or go? There was no decision. Dr Claire Bannon was going home.

CHAPTER FOUR

THE slow drive home was more enjoyable than Claire had envisaged. The roads were treacherous, with recent snowfalls covering icy surfaces, but Alastair drove well. The combination of the luxurious leather upholstery, superb heating and the prospect of surprising her family combined to relax her taut nerves.

Alastair concentrated on his driving and for a while there was silence. Claire tried to keep her attention on the scenery, but every now and then her eyes would stray to the man beside her. He was good-looking, she decided. Without the beard and in a dinner suit he would be magnificent. As it was. . . She studied the beard and the well-cut tweed jacket. He looked rugged and capable, as if there was little in life Alastair Drummond wouldn't be able to deal with.

His eyes suddenly swung from the road in front and, for a fraction of a second, met hers. His expression of concentration lifted to amusement. Claire blushed a deep crimson and turned away. When she next ventured a quick glance across the amusement was still there.

'This is a lovely car,' she said tentatively.

'It is, isn't it?' he agreed gravely. 'Unfortunately it doesn't belong to me. My boss is skiing in Switzerland and lent it to me for a couple of weeks.'

'Your boss? You're not a tourist, then?'

'No.'

Silence.

'Well?' demanded Claire with asperity. 'If you're going to bulldoze your way into my Christmas you might at least tell me something about yourself.'

'Sorry, ma'am.' He grinned. 'Just keeping my place.'

'Oh, cut it out!' She returned the grin in spite of herself and the tension eased. 'You're a doctor of medicine?'

He flashed her one of his heart-stopping smiles.

'I thought we'd settled that. . .' He negotiated a stretch of deep snow in silence.

Claire sat quite still, while Alastair concentrated on his driving.

'Then when I ordered you out of the way——' She broke off. 'Oh, no.'

Alastair smiled.

'No worse than me ordering you to get out of the way. And even if you'd known, there was every justification for you to take over. I was in no condition to be treating anyone.'

Claire shook her head.

'I'm sorry.'

'Don't be.' Alastair's disarming smile flashed across at her.

She looked across at him curiously. 'What do you do in Australia? And what are you doing here?'

'I run a practice at Gimboral, a tiny country town about twenty miles from the coast in western Victoria. I run a solo practice, not through choice, but because finding doctors prepared to work in small country towns in Australia is almost impossible. When I went into the practice I had a partner who was skilled in obstetrics. I've got my surgical qualifications, so the two of us worked well together. Since he's retired I've been forced into both jobs and, frankly, I didn't know enough. Ninety-five per cent of babies make it with no help whatsoever, but when they do need help they deserve more skill than I had. I was lucky enough to find a locum prepared to take over for four months and have spent the time delivering as many babies as Professor Pennington will allow. He's one of the top obstetricians in this country, and I jumped at the chance to study with him.'

'You've been here for four months?'

'Yes. Officially I've finished. Thanks to the professor lending me his car, though, I've decided to take a couple of weeks to see the sights before I go home.'

'And then you're heading back to Gimboral to deliver all the local babies for the rest of your life?'

Alastair laughed. 'You make it sound as if there are thousands of them. I'd be lucky if I got one a fortnight. I've got another problem in that I still need a partner. It's dangerous to deliver babies without the capacity to do a Caesarian, and for that I need another doctor who can give an anaesthetic. The practice is big enough to support a partner, but it's difficult to persuade young doctors that a country practice can be rewarding.' He looked over at her and grinned. 'You don't fancy a move, do you?'

Claire shook her head with a laugh. 'It's a bit far from home for me, thank you very much.'

'You can't say I don't try.' He returned the smile. 'It really is a great spot. I started practising there five years ago and would never go anywhere else. Mind you,' he paused reflectively, 'I'm biased—I grew up there. My parents had a property a few miles from Gimboral. My mother still lives there.'

They fell silent again, the silence broken only by the

slushing sound of the car driving smoothly through the snow.

'Your turn.'

'Pardon?'

'Your turn, Dr Bannon. Tell me about yourself.'

She shook her head.

'There's not a lot to tell. I work too hard to be interesting. I grew up on a little farm in the Dales, went to school, started nursing and then decided to do medicine instead. I've had my nose to the grindstone ever since.'

'Do you enjoy it?'

'I love it,' she confessed. 'It's meant a lot of sacrifice for my family, though, and I mean to prove to them that it's been worthwhile.'

'How long since you graduated?'

'Three years.'

'And you've been working at St Mark's since then?'

'Mm.'

They chatted easily. Claire found herself telling him about her work. He listened as though he was really interested, throwing in a question here and there, commenting on the standards of training, comparing her experiences with his training in Melbourne. He was a good listener, and Claire found herself talking much more than was usual for her.

'Do you still enjoy working at St Mark's?' he asked at the end of her résumé of the work she had been doing.

Her voice grew thoughtful. 'It's terrific experience.'

'But you're not sure you want to spend the rest of your life in a hospital job?' Alastair asked.

Claire flushed.

'I'm not sure.' She shook her head. 'I'm not sure.'

'Afraid to stretch your wings?'

'No,' she retorted crossly. 'Have you finished the interrogation?'

'Well,' he looked across at her consideringly, 'I would like to know how you got the limp.'

'Limp?'

'The one you wear on your right leg,' Alastair said patiently.

'You noticed?'

'I'm a doctor, remember? I'm trained to notice.'

Claire shook her head and said nothing.

'A car accident?' The voice was gentle but insistent.

'Yes.'

'A bad one?'

'Yes.'

'Want to tell me about it?'

'No.'

Instead of saying anything he flashed her an amused look, then concentrated on the road ahead. Claire shifted restlessly in her seat. The sudden compulsion to tell him was inexplicable.

'It was when I was seventeen. I was training as a first-year nurse.' She bit her lip, but the compulsion was still there. 'My boyfriend persuaded me to pretend I was sick and take a day off.'

'And?'

'Mark had been drinking before he picked me up—I didn't know until afterwards. All I know is that he was showing off, speeding, trying to scare me a little, I guess. He went over a crest too fast and there was a lorry coming the other way. The lorry driver didn't stand a chance.'

'He was killed?'

'Yes. So was Mark. I spent months in hospital and ended up with one leg a bit shorter than the other.'

'And different in other ways too.' It was a statement, not a question.

'Yes.' She looked at him steadily. 'I've stopped wasting time. I started medical school and have tried to make up in some way for two wasted lives.'

'No more boyfriends?'

'What do you think?' she threw at him defiantly.

He shook his head. 'What a waste!'

Claire bit her lip. She concentrated on her hands, lying restlessly in her lap. She felt rather than saw him glance at her.

'I'm sorry.' His voice was gentle.

'It's OK.'

'It's not.' He placed a finger across on her cheek and ran it slowly down to her lips. 'It's quite a load you're carrying around, little one.'

Claire flushed. 'Oh, for heaven's sake! Can we leave it?'

'Fine,' he agreed, much to her relief. 'Not another single question, I promise. It's your turn again. See if you can find some murky secrets in my past.'

She shook her head and relaxed as she leaned back against the leather upholstery.

This time the silence was companionable. Claire felt peaceful and strangely happy. Alastair flicked on the radio and the strains of Handel's *Messiah* echoed through the car. Merry Christmas, Claire told herself softly. She looked up and found Alastair's eyes on her face.

'Merry Christmas,' he said.

* * *

The farmyard gate was open. As the car pulled up outside the old stone house Claire closed her eyes, savouring the moment to come. Alastair sat watching with understanding. As she reached down to unclip her seatbelt she hesitated and looked up at him.

'Thank you for bringing me home. It means a lot to me.'

'I know—that's why I did it.' He paused. 'Would you like me to unload Frederick and Clarabel and leave?'

'Don't you dare.' She glared at him. 'Besides, you haven't had your gruel.'

'Neither I have.'

As he spoke the front door swung open. Her father appeared, shading his eyes with his hand as he tried to discern the visitors. With a squeal of delight Claire was out of the car and in his arms.

Christmas was magnificent. Claire's family greeted her with joy. Alastair, as the means of bringing their girl home to them, was welcomed with real pleasure, and soon found himself seated in the midst of Claire's nieces and nephews, assisting with doll dressing, helping with construction sets and answering interminable questions.

Frederick and Clarabel were greeted with teenage rapture, and once Aunt Lil recovered from the shock of first meeting her aspidistra she professed herself delighted.

'Are you sure?' Claire asked wickedly. 'Alastair wouldn't mind swapping it for you if you thought you'd like something larger.'

Alastair hurled a large cushion across the room at

her. Having heard the saga of the gifts the family howled her down in indignation.

By the time the last morsel of pudding had disappeared and the last gift was opened the light was fading. Alastair stood up, depositing a small cousin on to the floor.

'It's getting late. Thank you all for making me so welcome. It's time, though, that I was leaving.'

He was greeted by general dismay. Claire's mother looked across at Claire, waiting for her daughter to signal her desire for him to stay.

Claire looked up from the train set she had been helping to operate. Alastair was standing almost directly above her. She looked around the room at her beloved family and a wave of gratitude swept through her. She started to her feet and a hand reached down to take hers. He pulled her up and steadied her, but made no move to let the hand go. Claire looked helplessly across at her mother and then up into the deep eyes solemnly watching her.

'Please stay,' she said shyly. 'That is, if we're not keeping you from some other celebration.'

His eyes met hers. They might have been alone in the room together.

'Would you like me to?'

Claire met the look.

'I would like you to. Besides,' she smiled, 'we still haven't given you your gruel.'

Her mother had waited only for her signal before joining the general protestations. The rambling old house could easily accommodate another. The thing was settled, and Claire was left with the confused feeling of not knowing whether she was glad or sorry.

* * *

She woke in the early hours of the last day of her break with the odd sensation that something had woken her. She opened her eyes and strained to listen, but could hear nothing. She glanced at her watch. Three a.m. Deciding she had been mistaken, she snuggled down on to her pillows. Another five or so glorious hours of sleep with no insistent alarm at the end of it. If she was lucky her mother would wake her with a cup of tea and she would be allowed to snooze some more.

The last couple of days had been fun, she decided sleepily. Alastair had fitted in as if he had known them all his life instead of two short days. He had been keen to find out all about the farm, and her father had recognised a kindred spirit. Last night he had even won the greatest accolade—he had been allowed to help with the milking. All Claire's offers to help in the past had been met with a curt,

'Get away, girl. You'll make them skittish.'

Claire's father brooked no strangers in his dairy, and Claire shook her head in disbelief when she realised where Alastair was.

The family were watching her and Alastair closely, she knew. They had worried about her since her accident. She didn't fit the mould they knew or understood. They were an attractive family, and the other girls had brought home a succession of eager boyfriends. With Claire there had been no one since Mark and now they held their breath and waited. Even Auntie Lil, who usually hurried home to her three cats and her budgie as soon as she decently could, had said to Claire's mother,

'You know, Mary, I might just stay on for a wee while this year, if it's all the same with you. Mrs Thomas will feed the cats for me.' Her eyes had been on Alastair as she spoke, and Claire knew her inquisitive mind was alight with curiosity.

She was given no food for gossip. Claire steered a course as far from Alastair as she could manage, not really understanding her reasons for doing so. Her life up to now had been free of emotional entanglements, and that was the way she intended it to stay. At seventeen she had thought she was in love with Mark, intelligent, fun-loving Mark who took every ounce of pleasure life held out for him. Well, Mark was dead, his promising career as an engineer cut short, and Claire was left with the memory of what could happen when responsibilities were forgotten. It wouldn't happen again. She had promised herself that somehow she would atone for those two wasted lives. Somehow. Her mother said she worked hard enough for two, and that was just what she intended doing for the rest of her life. Romance was for others.

If only Alastair didn't have the effect of making her feel like a gauche schoolgirl. He had promised to drive her back today, and she was alternately anticipating and dreading the time in the car with him.

She was not looking forward to returning to the hospital. The break had made her realise how truly weary she was. Three hours was a long way from her family. Perhaps she should consider general practice. If she enquired there might be a possibility of a position closer to home. She thought briefly about Alastair's problem, and smiled to herself. General practice in Australia? He had to be joking!

Claire's sister was due to have a baby in a fortnight, and with two little ones already she was tired to the point of exhaustion. Perhaps I'll apply for leave when Jill has the baby, thought Claire. I could look after the

little girls and look around for another position while
I'm home. With that comforting thought she snuggled
back into the pillows.

A stifled cry from the room next door made her eyes
spring open again. Jill and her husband Rob were
sleeping next door, and Jill was eight and a half months
pregnant. Claire sprang out of bed and grabbed her
robe.

Jill was alone in the room, crouched over on the side
of her bed. She didn't look up as Claire entered. One
look was enough to ascertain she was mid-contraction.
Claire waited until the contraction passed and then
gently eased her back on to the bed.

'Where's Rob?' she asked.

Jill grimaced and then gave her a weak smile.

'He's gone to ring the hospital. It's been snowing so
hard he's reluctant to take me without checking that
we can get through. I'm not all that partial to having
this baby in the back of the Morris.'

'I don't blame you.' Claire crossed to the window
and looked down. The lights were on downstairs,
throwing thin shafts of light from the bottom windows.
Snow was falling heavily and a thick blanket covered
the ground. She turned back to Jill to discover her in
the grip of another contraction. Two minutes apart.
Even if the road was clear she would be lucky to make
it. She waited until the pain eased and then sat by the
bed.

'How do you feel about a home birth?'

Jill tried to smile, but it didn't quite come off.

'Have I a choice?'

'Home or the Morris, by the look of it.'

Rob opened the door and came in behind them. His
face cleared as he saw Claire.

'Thank God you're here, Claire! I've just been through to the hospital and they say there's no way. They'll send an ambulance as soon as they can get through, but by the sound of it we're on our own.'

'There wasn't any problem with the last two, was there, Jill?'

'No.' The reply was terse.

'Well, then—no problem.' Claire gave her most reassuring smile, hoped it made them feel better than it did her and packed Rob off for towels.

The time passed slowly. Claire made all the necessary preparations for what she hoped would be a straightforward delivery and waited. It should be all right. She had no equipment and little experience to deal with anything out of the ordinary, but this was Jill's third child. She sat and waited, reassuring her sister and chatting to Rob.

An hour later the little confidence she possessed had slipped. What Claire wanted was a brightly lit labour ward, proper equipment and above all a specialist obstetrician at call. All she had was her stethoscope, and the news that was giving her was not good. As Jill started feeling the urge to push Claire examined her. She was fully dilated and ready to go. Twenty minutes later nothing was happening, and Jill was getting increasingly distressed. Claire listened to the foetal heart beat and straightened. She needed help.

'Will you get Alastair?' she whispered to Rob.

'It's not good, is it?'

'The baby should be here.' Her eyes were on Jill's face as she spoke, her voice lowered to be out of Jill's hearing. She didn't add that the baby's heart was faltering. Rob had already gone.

Alastair was in the room in two minutes, buttoning

his shirt as he entered. It was all Claire could do not to burst into tears on his chest as he appeared. She didn't feel like a doctor. It was her sister in trouble, and her medical training was no use at all. It told her what was wrong. Without equipment she was powerless to do anything about it, even if her hands would stop shaking long enough for her to do so.

Alastair assessed the situation at a glance and crossed immediately to the dressing-table, where Claire had bowls of hot, soapy water and clean towels. He scrubbed scrupulously, listening to Claire's account of the labour as he did so. As he finished Rob returned, bearing a large black case.

'Thanks, Rob.' Alastair indicated the chair beside the bed and Rob put down the case.

'You haven't got equipment?' Claire held her breath.

'I hope so. I'm driving the professor's car, remember. His bag was still in the back, so with a bit of luck we'll have what we need. It's fortunate I didn't take it out to give Frederick and Clarabel more room.' Rob flicked the bag catch and Alastair let out a sigh of satisfaction as he checked the contents. 'Good old Professor. A complete obstetric kit.' He turned back to the bed, speaking softly to Jill as he did so.

'For some reason, this baby's got himself a bit stuck. You don't mind if I give him a bit of assistance, do you?'

Jill's answer was unintelligible. She had grabbed Rob's hand and was holding on for all she was worth.

Alastair deftly made an examination, then took Claire's stethoscope and listened. His face set as he did so, and Claire bit her lip. It wasn't her imagination.

As he examined Jill, Claire was also checking the case. By the time he had finished she had prepared a syringe. She handed him the injection of local anaesthetic and turned back to find the tools he would need for an episiotomy.

The forceps were there, nestled in their own sterile bag. As Claire handed them to Alastair she took the stethoscope and placed it low on Jill's tummy. Her eyes widened in panic. The soft, fluttering heartbeat could only just be heard. She looked up at Alastair and he read the message in her eyes. Swiftly they moved Jill into position and Alastair applied the forceps.

He was skilled. Claire had done forceps deliveries before, but there was no way her skills matched his. The thought came unbidden into her mind. Perhaps I could work with him. There was no fumbling. The forceps were fitted on their target, a wait until the contraction reached its peak and then a gentle turn and pull. The baby's head came into view. Another contraction and the head was clear. Before the next contraction could deliver the baby completely Alastair was clearing the airway, working on giving this baby a chance.

The next two minutes were grim. There was absolute silence in the room as Alastair fought for the tiny new life. Claire turned to Jill, making sure she was recovering. Behind her Alastair breathed for the little boy, his mouth almost covering the tiny face. Claire delivered the placenta and mechanically collected the equipment to start sewing the episiotomy. There was no sound behind her. Jill kept her tight hold of Rob's hand and the dreadful wait continued.

They heard the breath first, an infinitesimal suck of air magnified in the stillness. A moment afterwards a thin wail echoed through the room, and Claire closed her eyes in silent thankfulness. On the bed, Jill started to cry.

Twenty minutes later Alastair and Claire left the room to find a reception committee waiting in the passage. Even Auntie Lil was there, her head bedecked with curlers and her face wreathed in smiles. In her arms Claire held the newest addition to the family, by now soundly asleep.

After crooning over the reason for all the fuss the family gradually dispersed, leaving Alastair and Claire with Claire's mother and father.

'I'm just so grateful you were home,' Mrs Bannon said to Claire.

'It wasn't me, Mum.' Claire shook her head. 'If it weren't for Alastair this little one wouldn't have made it.' She looked down at the bundle in her arms. 'Have we got a crib somewhere? I'll pop him in my room tonight and let Jill have some sleep.'

Her mother hurried off to search the attic. Her father grasped Alastair's hand and shook it.

'Thanks, lad. You've done our family a service we'll not forget in a hurry.' He turned to Claire and grinned wickedly. 'If I were you I'd marry him, miss. It seems the family could use two doctors!' He disappeared, chuckling to himself.

Claire gazed after him, her face crimson, then turned back to Alastair. 'I can manage now.'

'I'll stay while you settle him. After all, he's my patient.'

Claire's mother returned, bearing an ancient white bassinet.

'It's done all this lot,' she said happily as she set it up in Claire's bedroom. 'I knew it would come in handy if I just kept it long enough.' Claire lowered the sleeping baby and stood soaking in the tiny miracle. Her mother bustled off to bed. Alastair stayed, watching aunt and nephew.

Finally Claire turned to him and held out her hands.

'Thank you, Alastair.'

He took the outstretched hands and stood looking down at her.

'My pleasure.' He didn't let go of the hands. 'Claire?'

'Yes?'

'Your father talked about marriage. How do you feel about a partnership?'

Claire gasped and pulled back from his grasp.

'Don't be ridiculous!'

A smile lurked behind the deep green eyes. 'Would I joke about something this serious?'

'Wh—what do you mean by partnership?' she stammered.

The smile deepened. 'Perhaps not what your father intended.' His finger traced the contour of her cheek. 'Although even that could eventuate, given a certain lady's change of heart. What I'm saying at the moment is that I need help. Gimboral is a little town desperate for a doctor and Claire Bannon is a trained doctor ready for a change. What about giving it a go?'

'Come to Australia, you mean?'

'Come to Australia.'

'You're mad.'

He grinned and said nothing.

Claire looked up at him with indignation. 'It's three in the morning. I've just been through a hair-raising experience. I've got a new nephew and a perfectly good job and you lay a crazy proposition like this before me!'

'It's not the proposition I'd like to lay before you,'

he admitted. 'If I gave you the one which more readily springs to mind you'd probably show me the door.'

Claire drew in her breath. 'Get out!'

He smiled. 'Claire, take me seriously for a moment. It's a demanding job I'm throwing at you. At least pay me the courtesy of thinking about it.'

'I'm thinking. Get out!'

'Is that what you really want?'

'Out!'

He shook his head, the smile still lurking deep behind the green eyes. 'Guard your heart, Claire Bannon. It's in danger.' His laughing eyes held her. Before she knew what he was about he reached out for her, swinging her up against him. His mouth found hers.

Ignoring her protests, he kissed her hard, his mouth searching, demanding. His tongue pushed past her stiff lips, seeking the moistness beyond. Strong arms pulled her unresponsive body firmly into him, forcing her to feel his might, his sheer male potency. She moved to push him away, but her strength was no match for his. She was locked against him until such time as he was willing to relinquish his captive.

His tongue found an opening and started its careful exploration of the deep warmth of her mouth. The brutal push of his tongue ceased, and his movements softened, gentled. Down her back his open fingers played with her spine, feeling her form beneath the soft folds of her robe.

Her futile struggles faltered and ceased. With amazement she felt her body move to his, stirring with tremors of warmth and fire. Her lips parted fully, her hands came up to feel the strength of him, the muscled tautness of the arms that held her.

What was she doing? A shaft of sanity pierced her trembling body and with a jerk she pulled back. Their eyes stayed locked. The laughter had faded from his face. His look was serious, almost stern.

'Give yourself a chance, Claire.'

She shook her head angrily, pulling out of his grasp.

'Get out of this room!' Her voice was a sob. She didn't trust him. She didn't trust herself.

Alastair smiled faintly. 'Never let it be said that I can't take a hint. Goodnight, little one.' He reached out and touched her lips lightly, then turned to the sleeping baby. 'Goodnight, sir. Look after your Auntie Claire for me. I've got work for her to do.' He left.

Claire was left staring blindly at the closed door. Beside her, in the crib, the little boy opened his eyes and gazed uncomprehendingly at a strange new world.

CHAPTER FIVE

MELBOURNE, Australia. Claire gazed from the window in the plane to the country below. How could this be a major city? The plane was approaching Tullamarine, Melbourne's international airport, and yet underneath were open fields. Paddocks, Claire corrected herself. Australia had paddocks.

What else did Australia have? She was about to find out. All she knew at the moment was that somehow, against her reason and her better judgement, she had been talked into a job as general practitioner at Gimboral. Gimboral, of all places! Her school atlas had never heard of it. Nobody had ever heard of it. In the last few weeks, as she had resigned her job, negotiated her Australian medical registration and packed her suitcases, she had had moments of questioning her sanity. How on earth had Alastair talked her into it?

The long drive home after Christmas was responsible. Claire had started the drive angry and suspicious. Three hours later she had agreed to give the job a try.

Alastair had spoken seriously, carefully avoiding any personal implication. He had outlined the job as a challenge, something she could put all her efforts into.

'We need you, Claire,' he had said, his countenance grave. 'You've got the training I've been looking for in a partner. You're skilled and yet you're ready to ask for help when you need it. We could work well together.'

Claire had cast a suspicious glance at him, but he had remained serious.

'Come and give it a try. At worst it would be excellent general practice experience. At best,' he cast her a sidelong look, 'well, who knows?'

Who knows, indeed? thought Claire. Alastair was right, though, in that she did need a change. He was a skilled general practitioner and surgeon. His combination of skills meant that he had a lot to teach her and, given the isolation of Gimboral, she would be forced to learn. It would be a responsible and demanding job, with no specialists waiting in the wings to take over when things became difficult. Could she be sure their contract would be purely professional, though? It would be up to me to ensure it stayed that way, she thought. I'm not about to let my heart rule my head.

Claire's family, to her surprise, were delighted with her decision.

'You'll come back to get married, though,' Jill ordered as Claire dropped in to say goodbye to her newest nephew.

'Jill!' expostulated Claire. 'Cut it out. I'm going to try my hand at general practice and to see Australia. Marriage is fine if you're cut out for it, but I'm not. I'm going to Australia to work.'

Jill just grinned and moved the baby to her other breast.

'We'll see.' She addressed herself to the downy little head. 'We'll see whether Auntie Claire is as hard-hearted and professional as she thinks she is, or whether a certain Dr Drummond might have other ideas.'

The little boy ignored her, intent as he was on a task of much more importance than his Auntie Claire's

love-life. Claire was grateful for his indifference. He
was the only member of the family not showing an
entirely unwarranted interest in Alastair Drummond.

So now, six weeks later, she was descending to land
in Australia. 'You're crazy,' she told herself. I agree, a
little voice at the back of her head answered back.

The 747 landed with a shudder, then settled for the run
to the terminal building. Claire collected her belongings and tried to calm herself. She realised she was
shaking, and there was no way she could blame that on
the cold. As she emerged into the tunnel leading from
the aircraft the heat struck her with almost physical
force. February was the hottest month in Australia,
she had been told. She didn't see how it could get much
hotter. She made her way along the tedious Customs
queue, then through the doors into the main terminal
building.

He wasn't there.

Claire felt a surge of desolation. She put down the
cases and chided herself. It was ridiculous to expect to
be met. She was coming out to take up a job. Naturally
Alastair would expect her to make her own travel
arrangements.

'Could Dr Claire Bannon come to the Qantas reception desk, please?' The voice blared over the public
address system, causing her to close her eyes in
momentary thankfulness. She wasn't completely isolated. She picked up the big cases and made her way
forward. A smiling receptionist handed her a note.

'Unavoidably detained. Wait. Alastair.'

Claire stood staring at the stark words. She'd come
halfway across the world to be met by this! With a sigh

of sheer weariness she limped across to a quiet corner of the terminal building and sat.

She attracted a few curious glances as she settled on one of the numerous benches. Her dark, glossy hair accentuated the pallor of her face and the shadows under her huge eyes. Her soft cream suit seemed too old and sophisticated for such a waiflike figure.

Three hours later Alastair found her. She was curled up, lost in sleep on the hard vinyl seat. For a long moment he stood looking down at her, until she sensed his presence and opened her eyes.

'Alastair.'

'Claire,' he said softly.

She struggled to a sitting position, momentarily confused. 'You came,' she said stupidly.

'Did you think I wouldn't?'

He reached down and seized her hands, drawing her up against him. For a moment they looked at each other, then he lifted her right off the ground and his mouth found hers. For a moment her resolutions were forgotten. The coarseness of his beard brushed her skin, sending prickles of desire through her. Her arms came up and wound around his neck, pulling him closer. They might have been alone together, instead of among crowds of travellers, many of them casting amused, sympathetic glances at the handsome couple so lost in the joy of meeting.

Gently they drew apart. Alastair searched her face.

'Tears, little one?'

'I'm not a "little one",' Claire retorted defiantly, pulling herself together. 'I'm just tired.'

'I'm sure you are.' His voice was full of tender amusement. 'I'm sorry. I had a child with a ruptured appendix just as I was about to set off. With no other doctor at Gimboral I can't operate until an anaesthetist arrives from Hamilton. By the time we operated it was a nasty piece of surgery. I had to stay until I knew he'd be OK.'

'And he will be?'

'Mm.' He nodded. 'It was closer than I'd like his parents to know, though. Never mind.' His tone was suddenly exultant. 'It's the last time I'll have to wait. I have my own resident anaesthetist now. Welcome to Australia, Dr Bannon.'

His lips gently brushed her forehead, then he picked up her suitcases and guided her to the door. Claire made her way to the car park, trying to suppress the niggle of doubt that had entered her tired mind. Would he be so pleased to see her if she weren't a doctor? She shook her head in irritation. This was stupid. It was she who wasn't interested in romance.

Claire slept for most of the drive to Gimboral. Seated beside Alastair in his big, comfortable car, she felt a release of the tension of the past few weeks. Every now and then she stirred and cast a glance at the bearded figure beside her. He was wearing casual trousers and a short-sleeved, open-necked shirt. The blond hairs showing at the V of his shirt spoke of masculinity and strength. He was so good-looking it wasn't fair, Claire thought. She blushed and resolutely closed her eyes again.

After a drive that lasted for most of the afternoon they finally reached Gimboral. Alastair woke her as they pulled into the town. Claire gazed around her, and marvelled that a town so small could support a hospital and two doctors. There were perhaps a dozen shops, a pub, a couple of churches set high on the hills overlooking the town and a little school. A bridge cut the town in two. A sign declared the miserable trickle of water to be the Wanden River.

'I'd hate to see what Australians term a stream,' thought Claire aloud.

'It's nearly dry,' Alastair explained. 'We've had a really nasty summer and are desperate for rain. In winter the Wanden's nearly two hundred metres across. It's never been known to dry up completely, though, and is the reason the town's here. It's still deep enough to be a satisfactory swimming hole and it gives us some security in the event of a grass fire.'

'Do you get many fires?'

Alastair grimaced. 'Too many for my liking, although there's only been one through the township in my lifetime. The town was burnt out about fifteen years ago.' He indicated one of the churches, a picturesque bluestone building. 'The Presbyterians rebuilt their church exactly as it was, using the same stone. There were a couple of houses that the fire jumped, but the rest of the town dates from fifteen years ago.'

'What do you mean when you say the fire jumped?'

Alastair shook his head. 'I've got no idea really. The fire just came through in a storm. Most of the locals got to the river in time, but there was no way they could save the houses. Buildings were actually exploding before the fire reached them with the intensity of the heat. Other places, perhaps little wooden houses that you'd swear would be the first to go, had a hedge planted just in the right position, or in some cases the fire just seemed to jump over them.'

'Was your farm burnt?'

'No. We're a few miles out and the fire missed us completely. That's not to say we'll always be as lucky, but we can hope. We haven't had a local fire yet this summer, touch wood. The country's as dry as tinder.'

He watched her as she continued to gaze around her. She shook her head in disbelief. It was a tiny settlement rather than what she knew as a town.

'How on earth do you get enough patients to run a hospital?' she finally blurted out. 'This place isn't a town.'

He grinned. 'Believe it or not, Dr Bannon, it really is a town. We may not look much, but Gimboral is the centre for a large rural area.'

'But the farms are all huge. I can't believe that this place ever gets busy.'

'The farms to the north of Gimboral are big,' Alastair agreed. 'It's a funny area. The highway marks the line where decent rainfall stops. North of the highway the rainfall is low and undependable. Farms can only carry sheep or beef cattle, so the farms are big. Five hundred hectares is a normal size holding. South of the highway as you get towards the coast the rainfall improves dramatically and it becomes dairy country. There you get much smaller farms and a denser population. It's from there that Gimboral gets most of its trade.'

While they had been talking the big car had headed across the bridge and pulled up outside the Gimboral hospital, a neat white building set back among English trees and manicured lawns. The hospital was an oasis in a scorched landscape, and Claire reacted with delight.

'We use bore water to keep the lawns going in summer,' Alastair explained. 'Water's precious, but the town agrees that the hospital garden is a priority. We have quite a few elderly patients who are here long-term. The garden's a special place for them, probably more important to them than the medicines I prescribe.'

'It's lovely,' Claire agreed.

'Come on.' He was out of the car and around opening her door. 'If you're not too tired I'll show you around.'

'With my sleep in the airport and again in the car I can't really complain.' Claire unwound from the leather upholstery and stretched her legs, wincing at the movement. She looked up to see Alastair watching her sympathetically.

'Bad?'

'No.' She shook her head. 'It really only hurts when I've been standing for a long time or sitting in the one position. The time spent in the plane has made it ache.' She concentrated on not limping as they entered the hospital. She didn't want sympathy here.

The contrast between St Mark's, a huge city hospital, and Gimboral Bush Nursing Hospital was amazing. Claire's overwhelming impression was of friendliness and curiosity. Patients and the nursing staff all seemed to know each other personally, and Alastair seemed to be on first-name terms with all of them. As he performed introductions he added personal comments.

The sister who came to greet them as they entered the hospital was a little dumpy woman with a wide, welcoming smile.

'This is Matron Wise, Claire, officially known as Peggy. Peggy has a farming husband and five teenage sons. She depends on this job to keep them in football boots.'

Peggy reached out and gripped Claire's hand.

'Lovely to have you here, Claire. You're very welcome. We've needed you for a long time.'

Claire returned the clasp, reassured by the warmth of the welcome. Peggy and Alastair were obviously old friends, chatting and giving each other cheek as Peggy accompanied them on a tour of the wards.

'This is Ray Chandler, Claire,' Alastair said as he ushered her into a private room near the entrance. 'He's suffering a broken ankle, bruises and wounded dignity. His sons have been telling him to fit roll bars to the tractor for years, and now they're saying I told you so.'

The elderly man grinned up at them from his mound of pillows.

'Young know-alls! What do they know about farming? If they had their way I'd have every fool modern contraption known to man.'

'Always the way with these youngsters,' Alastair agreed gravely. 'How old are the boys now, Ray? Both in their fifties now, aren't they?'

'Plenty of time for them to learn a little wisdom,' Peggy volunteered with a staight face, and the old man broke into a delighted chuckle. 'He wants to go home,' Peggy added, addressing Alastair. 'He seems to think we're not looking after him properly.'

Alastair looked down at the frail figure on the bed. 'You're on your own now, Ray, aren't you?'

'Yep.' The old man nodded. 'Ever since Edie died I've looked after meself. The boys want me to live with them, but I'm happy enough where I am. Grandchildren are OK if you can send 'em home to their parents at the end of the day, is what I reckon.'

'Well, we send them home here,' Alastair said firmly. 'You'd better let Peggy look after you for another few days or you're going to offend her sensibilities—and when Peggy's offended, we all suffer, believe me! Do you think you can put up with us a while longer?'

They left him chortling to himself as he settled down to his hospital dinner.

'A darn sight better for him than the baked beans he'd make for himself. He's got three sons and they've all got wives, but he might as well be a bachelor for all the care they take of him,' Peggy said darkly.

'I think they do all they're allowed to,' Alastair commented. 'He's got a lot of pride.'

Claire glanced up at him curiously. There was genuine affection in his voice. How did a doctor cope with knowing patients so well? In many ways there would be advantages, but in other areas she could see enormous problems in not being able to be dispassionate. Tragic death would hit home so much harder when you lived in a tight-knit community. Medicine here was going to have very different demands from medicine in the city.

They stopped in to check Alastair's little appendix patient. He was still heavily sedated. His mother, seated beside the bed, looked almost worse than the little patient, and Claire's heart went out to her. They checked the sleeping form, and Claire was relieved to see there were no set-backs. Alastair was able to totally reassure the mother. They left her with a lighter expression on her face, but there was no way she would leave her son for the night. They left Peggy setting up another bed for her in the room, so perhaps she could get some sleep as well.

After the hospital itself Alastair took Claire over to the clinic. There were two identical consulting-rooms with a pleasant reception area. A small surgery for minor procedures was down the hall, opposite a well furnished tea-room.

'The waiting-room hasn't been big enough, and if you think the tea-room looks new it's because I never have time to use it,' Alastair explained. 'I hope with two of us we'll cut down the waiting time.'

Claire was delighted. Her room was light and airy, painted in soft pastel shades with comfortable chairs for both doctor and patient. It was a far cry from the spartan examination cubicles of St Mark's. The rooms gave her the urge to start work.

'When do I begin?'

'Tomorrow, if you like,' Alastair smiled, 'although I thought you might like to have a couple of days to look around.'

'Tomorrow it is,' Claire said firmly.

As they emerged from the clinic a nurse came out of the hospital building in front of them. She was in her late twenties, Claire guessed, tall, striking and immaculately groomed. A lady used to getting her own way, was Claire's initial impression as she waited for Alastair's introduction.

'This is Rowena MacMillan, Claire. She's a sister here and also a family friend. Rowena's family own land near ours, and I've known her since she was knee-high to a grasshopper.'

Rowena flashed Alastair a gorgeous smile, displaying even, pearl-white teeth.

'Welcome to Gimboral, Dr Bannon. I'm sorry I wasn't here to meet you.' She threw a sympathetic glance to Alastair as if apologising for not being there to support him. 'I've only just come on duty.'

Claire took the outstretched hand, suddenly conscious of her travel-stained appearance.

'Can I leave you to give Claire a cup of tea, Rowena?' asked Alastair. 'I left in a hurry this morning and left paperwork undone. If I don't catch up now I'll forget. I shouldn't be long, then I'll take Claire out to the farm.'

'To the farm?' Claire queried.

'If it's OK with you I thought you could stay for a while with my mother and me,' Alastair replied. 'There are no living quarters attached here, and our place is big. My mother would enjoy the company for a while too. Of course, as you settle you can make what living arrangements you like.'

Claire flushed. She wasn't too sure about the arrangement, but it seemed she had no choice. Aware of Rowena's eyes watching her curiously, she nodded agreement. They stood watching his departure, then Rowena ushered her into the hospital staff-room.

'Do you live on a farm as well?' she asked Rowena.

'Oh, yes.' Another beautiful smile. 'My parents have a little place just out of town adjoining Alastair's farm. It's convenient for me to still live there. It's close enough for me to come in to work, but I can still stable my polo ponies. Polo's quite a cult here,' she explained. 'Do you ride?'

'No—at least, not since I was a child.'

'Oh, of course not. I'm sorry, how stupid of me. I'd forgotten about your leg.'

Claire stiffened. 'Alastair told you about my leg?'

'Well, of course. Naturally we knew there had to be some reason for you to be willing to come here. Unless you're one of the polo set, Gimboral holds little attraction. We've been trying for years now to find another doctor.'

'And you thought I was willing to come because I was lame?'

'Well, I can understand it would be difficult for you to work in a job where you weren't given some consideration. You should have no problems here, though. We all intend to be very supportive. I'm sure if Alastair thinks you're capable of doing the job, then we do too.'

Claire found her teeth were clenched tight together. 'That's very nice of you, but there's no need. I was given no consideration in the three years I worked at St Mark's. I'm not incapacitated.'

Rowena nodded sympathetically. 'Good for you! We're all behind you. Now that Alastair's finally got someone here we intend to do our best to keep you.'

'Did Alastair go to England more on a recruiting drive than for training, then?'

'Oh, no.' Rowena's laugh tinkled. 'He very much wanted to do the obstetric course. Trying to find a doctor willing to come here was a secondary consideration, of course.'

'Of course,' Claire agreed tightly.

'He's charming, isn't he?' Rowena continued. 'He can be so persuasive, especially to the female species. And so attractive.'

'Do you find him so?' Claire asked curiously.

'Oh, well, I suppose you could say I have to.' Rowena smiled. 'At the moment I'm having too much of a good time to settle down, but I guess I'll finally say yes to him. Our lives are so compatible, after all.'

Claire nodded. 'I'm sure they are.'

By the time Alastair returned Claire was only sure of one thing: Rowena MacMillan was a lady whom she disliked. She pushed her angry thoughts aside. Whatever strategies Alastair had thought necessary to bring her here were irrelevant. This place needed another doctor, and despite Rowena's comments she was sure she was capable of filling the need.

She was quiet in the car on the way to Alastair's home, and he glanced curiously across at her.

'Tired, little one?'

'Tired,' she agreed. 'And my name is Dr Bannon.'

Alastair's home was about six kilometres from the town. They turned off the main road on to a gravel track, then continued until Alastair pulled up before a gate. The sign on the gate said 'Ardlethan'.

'Home,' said Alastair. 'OK, Claire—Aussie etiquette, lesson number one. The passenger always opens the gate.'

Claire climbed out, gazing in awe at the parched brown paddocks around her. How on earth could stock survive on this land? She said as much to Alastair.

'We don't expect your intensity of farming,' he answered. 'Eight to ten sheep per hectare is all this country can support. That's why the farms are so big.'

The house was set well back from the road, a low, gracious wooden building surrounded by generous verandas. A couple of dogs emerged to sniff Claire curiously as she emerged from the car, but there was no other sign of life.

'Meet Red and Rusty.' Alastair flicked his fingers, and the two dogs ceased their inspection of Claire and abased themselves in delighted welcome at his feet. 'My mother will be on the back veranda—it's cooler there in the evenings. I rang from the hospital to warn her we were on our way, so I'd imagine she'll have tea ready for us.' He pulled the bags from the car and started up the wide stone steps.

Claire paused on the top step and looked around. Through the scattered gums around the house all she could see was scorched paddocks. As far as she could see there was no other house.

'How big is your farm?' she queried.

'Standard size—about five hundred hectares.'

'And the MacMillans'? Rowena said you were neighbours.'

Alastair smiled. 'Well, that's a bit bigger. The MacMillans are what we call locally the squattocracy. They've got one of the oldest runs in the district, about four thousand hectares.'

A little place just out of town. Well, well! Claire shook her head before continuing.

'Do you run this place as well as your medical practice? No wonder you need a partner!'

'No.' He shook his head ruefully. 'Not possible, I'm afraid. My father was killed just as I finished medical school. It was a very difficult decision, whether to stay on and do my residency or come home and run the farm. I couldn't bear to think of the place being sold, and it would have broken Mum's heart. In the end Rowena came to the rescue. I stayed doing medicine, and we've leased most of our land to the MacMillans. Mum's still not all that happy with the arrangement, but it's enabled her to stay here. Come on through. She'll be waiting to meet you.' He left the suitcases at the top of the steps and gestured Claire to precede him around the veranda.

Claire's first impression of Mrs Drummond was her eyes—deep green eyes that mirrored her son's. They were set in an older face, weather-worn, lined with laughter, age and something else. Pain? She looked as if she had spent her life on the land. Her hands on the linen tablecloth were brown and workworn. Her hair, almost white, was coiled loosely into a casual knot at the back of her head. She was seated and made no attempt to rise as Alastair and Claire approached. With a shock Claire realised she was sitting in a wheelchair.

'Welcome to Ardlethan.' She manoeuvred the chair towards Claire and held out both hands in welcome. 'So you're Claire.' She eyed Alastair wickedly. 'I see what you mean.'

Claire flushed, and Alastair looked discomfited.

'Cut it out, Mum!'

Mrs Drummond smiled at him and turned back to Claire. 'You must be exhausted, child. Alastair, show Claire her room. When you've had a wash and freshened up we'll have tea out here, and then early bed for you, if I'm not mistaken.

Mrs Drummond could become a friend, Claire thought as she lay in bed that night waiting for sleep. The bedroom was big, airy and comfortable. The sumptuous three-quarter bed gave her no reason for not getting to sleep, but her sense of time was wrong. Too much had gone on in the last two days for her to settle. She lay, covered only by a sheet, the big ceiling fan whirring lazily above her.

Tea had been relaxed and friendly. Alastair and his mother had an easy relationship, obviously based on deep affection. Why was Mrs Drummond in a wheelchair? She would find out soon enough, she thought.

Sleep eluded her. It was the silence more than anything, she thought. After years of sleeping in medical residences, the total silence of an isolated farm was intense. Even in Yorkshire there was always a faint hum of distant traffic. Here the occasional chirrup of a cricket broke the stillness. Nothing else.

The telephone's shrill ring broke discordantly into the night, and Claire listened as Alastair walked down the passageway to answer it. In the silence she could hear the faint murmur of his voice and caught the last phrase: 'I'll be there in about twenty minutes.'

In decision she flung back the sheet and reached for a pair of jeans and light blouse. She pulled a hairbrush through her tousled curls and emerged to meet Alastair as he headed for the front door.

'What on earth are you doing up?' His tone was curt.

'I can't sleep. What's the call?'

'Gil Francis, a farmer a few kilometres out. It sounds like renal colic.'

Claire grimaced. 'Would I be in the way if I came?'

'It's two in the morning.'

'Not by my time clock, it's not. I've just changed time zones, remember. According to my head it's midday, and I'm wide awake.'

Alastair grinned. 'Well, it's more than I am! It's a straightforward call. You'll regret it tomorrow, but come if you like.'

The night was still and moonlit. The countryside was empty, almost eerie in its sparseness. Claire couldn't imagine doing these sorts of calls alone. As if he had read her thoughts, Alastair broke the silence.

'We'll have to work something out about night calls. I'm not happy about you doing house calls at this hour. I thought perhaps you could do the night calls to the hospital and I'd cope with the house calls. They work out about even.'

'Suits me.' Claire smiled up at him and caught his answering smile.

The farmhouse they eventually turned into was small and dilapidated. A couple of dogs set up a volley of barks as they strained on their chains. A beam of light streamed from the front door as a woman emerged to meet them.

'Oh, Doc Drummond, I'm so pleased to see you!' Her ample form moved forward, resplendent in crimson nightgown and pink curlers, and she reached out a hand to Alastair. 'Gil's been in awful pain. He wouldn't let me call you before this. He kept reckoning it was going to ease, but every time it did, it started up again within a few minutes, only worse. We didn't want to call you till morning, but he's really in agony. I dunno what it is.' Her face creased in anxiety.

'Let's have a look, Mrs Francis.' Alastair gestured briefly towards Claire, moving towards the front door at the same time. 'This is Dr Bannon—she arrived from England this morning and felt like a drive.' He grinned. 'I always thought the poms were a peculiar race.'

'Oh!' The woman's hand flew to her mouth. 'The new lady doctor we've all been waiting for—and me in my curlers and all! Oh, my dear, I'm so pleased to meet you. Two doctors! He's getting right royal treatment tonight, that's for sure.'

Claire smiled, but said nothing. She followed the other two into the bedroom at the front of the house.

There was no mistaking the diagnosis. The pain-racked figure on the bed was scarcely able to acknowledge their presence. Alastair slipped on a cuff, administered pethidine intravenously and waited until the worst of the spasm was over.

'You've got a kidney stone, Gil,' he said gently as the straining and contorting eased. 'By the time the next spasm comes the pethidine will be taking hold and it'll be easier. In a few minutes the pethidine will have the pain under control.'

They waited, watching the slight figure on the bed slowly relax. As the pethidine took hold Gil was finally able to acknowledge their presence.

'I'll give the ambulance boys a ring,' said Alastair. 'I want you in hospital for the rest of the night so we can keep the pain-killers topped up. Until we can get rid of that stone you're going to be in a bit of discomfort.'

'Is that what you call it?' The farmer managed a weak grin. 'And how do you intend to get rid of the stone?'

'With luck you'll do it yourself.' Alastair was packing his equipment back in his bag. 'We'll pour fluid into you until you'll think you're drowning and see if we can flush it out over the next twenty-four hours.'

'With beer?'

Alastair grinned. 'One shot of pethidine and the cure's miraculous! No, Gil, not with beer, not even a shandy. If you behave yourself we might stretch to weak black tea, or perhaps raspberry cordial as a special treat.'

Gil grimaced. 'And if that doesn't work?'

'The chances are high that it will.'

'And if not?'

'Well,' Alastair smiled up at Claire, 'you'll just have to let us go in and get it. I've got a partner now.' He gestured to Claire. 'Do you trust us?'

Gil Francis looked up at Claire and smiled shyly. 'I guess if Doc Drummond says it's OK, then it's OK by me.'

'Someone has to be brave enough to try the new doctor,' Claire agreed cheerfully. 'You look like a good guinea-pig to me. All the same,' she smiled, 'I'd concentrate on flushing the stone loose on your own. In the long run it means less time on raspberry cordial.'

She stayed chatting with Gil and his wife while Alastair contacted the ambulance and rang the hospital with instructions for Gil's admission.

'Let's hope that's the last call for the night,' Alastair said as they pulled out of the driveway. He glanced across at Claire. 'Still not tired?'

'No.' She was conscious of warmth and a feeling of contentment.

'I'll run you up to Mount Fyans. We call it a mountain, though how it qualifies I don't really know. It's the highest point hereabouts, however. With this moon we should be able to see almost to the coast.'

Claire cast him a doubtful look, then firmly put her hesitations aside. It was a magnificent night. She felt as if the night was part of a setting in which she didn't belong. It was a peculiar dream. Any minute now someone would come and wake her and she would head for the casualty department of St Mark's. Meanwhile, the dream could be indulged, perhaps even enjoyed.

As they neared the top of a sharp incline she took in her breath. The night was still and the full moon lit the landscape almost as if it were day. They could see for the horizon, flat, rolling land dotted every now and then with a homestead. The big red gums relieved the barrenness only slightly. Away to the south a slight irregularity of the horizon gave a hint at changing landscape.

'That's the coast,' Alastair explained as he pulled the

car off the road and stopped. 'When we manage some time off together, if ever, I'll take you down to Port Campbell and Peterborough for the day. The coastline there is spectacular.'

Claire was hardly listening, caught up in a private world of wonder. This was Australia. She was really here. Unheedingly she opened the door of the car and climbed out. She stood, caught in the stillness, catching the faint scent of the big gums.

'Any regrets?'

She was suddenly aware of Alastair behind her. His hands held her shoulders, his body formed a curve for her to lean against. For a moment she tensed, then relaxed, leaning gently back against him.

'Not yet.' She smiled. His body against hers gave her a feeling of safety, of being cherished and protected. Danger, she tried to tell herself, but her tired mind and body betrayed her. She would worry about danger at some other time. 'I've hardly had time to work them out. What about you?' It was a stupid question, she acknowledged to herself later, almost asking for trouble.

'No.' His voice was soft, husky with suppressed passion. 'Like you, not yet.'

His hand came up and ran through the silky strands of her hair, gently caressing her skin, catching a tiny group of hairs and running his fingers along their length. Claire felt faint tremors of pleasure pulsate through her scalp, electric to his touch. Her body leaned back into him, tremulously aware of his strength. His mouth came down and found a shoulder. He kissed her softly on the bare skin, his hand still moving through her hair, wringing sensations from her she hadn't known she was capable of. Her legs felt strange, as if they belonged to someone else. They couldn't move. The hand slipped down through the opening of her blouse, cupping the tautness of her breast. The flimsy lace of her bra did not impede the searching fingers. Her nipples stood erect to receive him, trembling under his touch.

Still she didn't move. Her body desired nothing more than to bask in the warmth, the night and the man behind her. I must be drugged, she thought hazily. This can't be happening to me. She tried to break out of the fog of confusion and desire. She pulled herself sideways and found herself being twisted around and pulled into him, into the lovely moistness of his mouth, into the coarseness of his beard and his hard, demanding body. She groaned with pleasure, her body as awake with desire as his. Her arms pulled his head down to hers, her tongue explored the roughness of his face, tasting him, wanting him. No man had ever had this effect on her. Oh, God, she was out of her depth. What was she doing?

In a surge of panic she pulled away, giving a whimper of pure terror. She backed away from him, like a frightened animal unsure of its surroundings. He made to follow, to take her again, but her hands came up to ward him off.

'No.'

He shook his head. 'Claire Bannon, stop kidding yourself.' His voice was not quite steady. 'You want me as much as I want you.'

'No!' It was a cry of anguish rather than denial. She took another step backwards and stumbled on the rough ground. His hands came out and caught her, steadying her. She snatched herself away and almost ran to the other side of the car. From the comparative safety of a car body distance she tried to regain some sort of control. Tears of anger and frustration welled in her eyes. She didn't understand this man, and her response frightened her. He was playing with her, and she didn't understand the rules.

'Take me home!' she muttered through gritted teeth. 'I've had enough. You don't have to keep this up. You've got me here now and I'll stay, regardless of the means you thought you had to employ to bring me here. For your information, they weren't necessary— in fact they had the opposite effect. You think you're so darned attractive that I just couldn't wait to get out here to you, but you're wrong, Alastair Drummond. I came here to work. So you can go happily back to your nice little romance or whatever you've got with Rowena MacMillan and leave me alone. I'm not here to play games.'

He stood and looked at her for an interminable moment, his eyes dark and unfathomable.

'Is that what you think?' His voice was tinged with anger. 'That I made love to you just to get you to come to Australia?'

'I don't know what your motives were in making love to me,' Claire snapped. 'All I'm saying is that I don't want it. Leave me alone!'

CHAPTER SIX

CLAIRE woke to the sound of laughing. Still half asleep, she raised herself on one elbow and stared in disbelief at the open window. A horrible, raucous laugh sounded not three metres from the room. Pushing herself out of bed, she padded across the polished floor to the window. The sound was dreadful, surely not human. She pulled back the lace curtains. Sitting on a low-hanging bough of a nearby gum-tree was a bird. A kookaburra! It eyed her speculatively as if saying,

'Oho, I've woken one up, then!' before launching into flight, probably to perform similar missions at other bedroom windows.

Claire grimaced. It was early yet, soon after dawn, she thought as she slipped back into the big, comfortable bed. She glanced at her watch. Six o'clock. She'd only been asleep for two hours. Surely there was plenty of time before she needed to stir. She lay back, trying to sort out the kaleidoscope of different impressions she'd had of this country and of the man she was going to work with. It was too much. Sleep enveloped her again.

When next she woke the heat was starting to permeate the house. Silence. It would take some getting used to, she thought, as she showered and dressed. It sounded as if she was completely alone in the house. She slipped into a soft cotton dress and matching sandals, caught her hair loosely back with slides and emerged from the bedroom. Still silence.

The living-rooms were deserted. Claire glanced out of the window. Alastair's car was gone. Guiltily she checked her watch: ten a.m. So much for starting work today! She opened the door leading to the kitchen. Mrs Drummond was seated at the big wooden table podding peas into a bowl in front of her.

'Good morning, dear.' Her smile was warm and welcoming. 'I didn't expect to see you until lunchtime.'

Claire shook her head in disgust. 'I'm sorry, I've overslept. You should have woken me.'

'There was no need.' Mrs Drummond pushed her chair back from the table and wheeled across to the bench. As Claire watched she set up two cups and reached for the big kettle on the slow combustion stove. She silenced Claire's involuntary protest with a gesture.

'You're a guest in my house this morning, child. Tomorrow, I'll let you get your own breakfast, but not this morning. I don't know what my son was doing, letting you traipse around the countryside with him last night. I've given him the rounds of the kitchen table, believe me!'

Claire grinned. She couldn't imagine this soft-spoken lady giving anyone the rounds of the kitchen table, much less a son whom she plainly adored. She was aware she was under close scrutiny.

'He did wear you out, didn't he? Those shadows are deeper than they were last night.'

Claire put a hand involuntarily to her face. She hadn't put on make-up, deeming it unnecessary in this heat, but now she wished she had.

'Don't worry,' Mrs Drummond said gently. 'They're not unbecoming. Certainly not worth running back to put make-up on.'

Claire flushed. 'How did you know that's what I wanted to do?'

'I'm a mind-reader, dear. Didn't Alastair warn you?'

Claire grinned and shook her head. 'That's it, then— I'm not staying in the same house as a mind-reader. I'm off to a hotel.'

'You'll have a hard time trying to find a hotel fit to stay in in these parts,' the elderly lady retorted. 'There's only the Commercial in Gimboral, and, although they're bound by law to offer accommodation, their standards are such that no one in their right mind would ever want to stay there. If you can bear us I'm afraid you're stuck with Alastair and me.' As she talked she placed a sliced grapefruit and a plate of hot buttery toast in front of Claire.

'Mrs Drummond, if you're going to look after me like this you'll have a lot of trouble getting rid of me, mind-reading or not,' Claire warned.

'Dorothy, please,' the lady begged. '"Mrs Drummond" still makes me think of my mother-in-law. Every time I hear it I get an urge to get up and dust the architraves.'

Claire smiled. Even if there were tensions between her and Alastair, at least with this lady she could relax. She finished her cup of tea and stretched in her chair, wincing a little as she did so. The enforced stillness of the hours in the plane had left her leg stiffer than it had been for years.

'Sore?'

Claire nodded unselfconsciously. She knew instinctively that there was no use in pretending to this woman.

'How did you do it?'

Claire told her the bare outlines, grateful for the fact

that Alastair had apparently not told everyone the full
story of her accident. At the end it seemed natural to
say,

'And you? How did you damage your legs?'

Dorothy's eyes met hers calmly. 'Isn't it odd how
some people can ask and you really resent their prying,
and others ask and you don't mind at all. Do you feel
like that?'

Claire nodded, remembering her acute dislike of
Rowena's knowing anything at all about her injury.

'Alastair was working as a resident in Melbourne.
Ross, Alastair's father, and I drove down to Melbourne
to see him. We were supposed to stay the night, but it
was hot and Ross was worried about fires here, so we
drove home. I've thought since then I would have
preferred a fire to raze the place rather than what
happened.'

'You had a car accident?'

'Yes. Ross drove home and I went to sleep beside
him. They say he had a heart attack and hit a tree, but
I still don't know whether it was the truth or if they
said it to make me feel less guilty. I should have stayed
awake. We'd had a lovely time and I was so happy and
contented. Driving home that night I thought everything was right with the world. And suddenly, everything wasn't.'

'And your legs?' Claire prodded gently.

'My spine was crushed. I was lucky to be alive, they
said, though for a long while I didn't believe that
either. Now. . .' Dorothy cleared the dishes to the
sink, manoeuvring her wheelchair expertly as she did
so. 'Now I don't rail against fate much any more except
in odd moments of depression or when Rowena
MacMillan reminds me of how helpless I am.' She

slapped a plate with a sudsy dish-mop and glared at it, as if conjuring up a vision of the lady mentioned.

Claire picked up a tea-towel and started wiping. She looked curiously at Dorothy.

'You don't like Rowena, then?'

'I do not.' The older lady pursed her lips and vented her spleen on the dishes for a few minutes. Claire dried in silence. Suddenly Dorothy looked up at her and laughed.

'Oh, goodness, child, I shouldn't be talking like this, but I'm going to anyway. Regard me as a patient who needs to talk, if you like, and invoke your professional code of ethics in keeping what I'm saying to yourself.'

Claire smiled and raised three fingers. 'Word of a Brownie. Come on—I'm dying of curiosity!'

Dorothy shook her head. 'There's no drama. I shouldn't say anything about Rowena because really she's been very good to us. Without her I guess we would have had to sell the farm, which would have been unspeakable.' She fell silent for a while. Claire finished drying up, then perched on a stool and waited for Dorothy to continue. Clearly she was aching for someone to talk to; her loneliness stood out like a beacon. Dorothy wiped the sink and picked up the peas again, toying with them as she spoke.

'Ross and I ran this farm as a team. I worked nearly as hard as Ross and we had it running magnificently. To look at it now you wouldn't recognise it for the same place.

'For about six months after the accident I wasn't good for anything. I was in hospital in Melbourne being "rehabilitated", and frankly I was in such a state I couldn't care less what became of this place. When I finally came home Rowena had it all organised. Her family were leasing the usable land for their sheep, all our lovely Hereford cattle had gone and she'd had the house renovated so I could operate a wheelchair in here. She'd even hired a housekeeper-companion for me. Alastair was so grateful, and so should I have been. I didn't have to do anything.' The voice was wistful.

'Except lie back and be an invalid?'

Dorothy looked gratefully up at Claire. 'You do understand.' Tears welled in her eyes and she brushed them aside impatiently. 'Ross and I ran this farm as it should be run. To sit back and watch the MacMillans swallowing it up is more than a body can bear.'

'But surely if it's leased you can reclaim it at any time?'

Dorothy smiled bitterly. 'Oh, no. Rowena's cleverer than that. She'll have it in the end.'

'When she marries Alastair?' The words sounded harsh. They echoed around the big kitchen, and Claire caught her breath. She shouldn't have said it. The older lady ceased fiddling with the peas in the basin before her and looked directly at her.

'Yes, that's her plan. She's been angling for Alastair since she was twelve years old. I often think that's the only reason she took up nursing. He's the only thing in her life that she hasn't been able to have for the lifting of her finger.'

'You're frightened of her, aren't you?'

'Yes.' Dorothy blew her nose defiantly. 'Well, given the same circumstances so would you be. Ever since the accident she's been here, helping Alastair and making subtle, helpful suggestions to him. He's so grateful to her. He can't see what she's trying to do, and everything I say sounds like sour grapes. Now she's

even suggesting it's cruel of him to expect me to stay
here by myself all day when I won't have the appalling
woman she employed as companion here. She thinks it
would be kinder in the long run to move me into a
nursing-home. The dreadful thing is that she makes all
my protestations sound as if I'm just staying here for
Alastair's sake. They'll have me in the local eventide
home before I know what I'm doing!' Dorothy caught
herself suddenly and looked ruefully down at her hand.
A rather squashed pea lay in her palm. 'Claire Bannon,
what must you be thinking of me? You've known me
for less than twenty-four hours and already you know
half the family secrets. I think I'd better banish you to
the Commercial after all.'

'I don't think I want to go any more,' Claire said
firmly. 'If you've finished pulping those peas perhaps
you could show me over the farm.'

The paddocks were hard and dry. Claire was amazed
where Dorothy could go with the chair. With a little
help and a specially fitted up four-wheel-drive vehicle
she could be back to running the place, Claire thought.
She certainly knew everything that was going on,
MacMillans or no MacMillans. She said as much to
Dorothy as she gave her a hand to push the chair over
the rough ground back to the house. Dorothy indulged
her by letting her help push, but Claire knew that
without her she was quite capable of doing it on her
own.

'Yes, well, I wish you'd mention it to Rowena's
father,' Dorothy said bitterly. 'He's got more money
than sense and always has had. He won't listen to a
thing I tell him, and I've stopped wasting my breath.
Look at these paddocks!' She gestured to the barren,

dusty plains. 'It shouldn't be as bare as this. We're not in the middle of a drought, no matter how hot it may seem to you. He's been overstocking. He's taking every ounce of goodness out of the soil and putting nothing back in. I suppose he's paying handsomely for the privilege and it's his prerogative, but the man's a fool.'

As they approached the house she gestured Claire over to the machinery shed.

'Over there, girl. There's something I want you to see.'

Standing under the corrugated-iron roof was an elderly Mercedes. It was dusty but had the air of a tried and trusty vehicle.

'Do you like it?' demanded Dorothy.

Claire looked at the big, solid body with its sober duco.

'It has the air of being a friend,' she said.

Dorothy laughed. 'I knew I was right about you.' She wheeled over to a workbench, groped underneath and produced some keys. 'Here.' She flicked them to Claire. 'This is my car. No, not the one Ross and I crashed, that was a write-off. Ross brought me this for our twentieth wedding anniversary. Alastair takes it out now and then to get rid of the cobwebs, but it's a lady's car. I'd like you to drive it while you're here.'

'You should be driving it yourself,' Claire said involuntarily.

'Yes, well, there's not a great deal of need for me to do that. Everything's done for me. Anyway, it's a manual transmission and I'd have to get it converted and special controls put in, besides learning to drive again without my legs. I guess I'm too old for that.'

Claire said gently, 'Dorothy, that's stupid.'

Dorothy shook her head. 'Not so stupid. Anyway, it

would give me a great deal of pleasure if I saw you drive it.'

'But what if I crashed it?'

'You won't. As you said, it's a friend. If Ross and I had been driving this instead of the new-fangled modern contraption he insisted on he'd still be here now. Besides,' Dorothy smiled up at Claire, 'you can't tell me you're not itching to get to that hospital. If you accept my very kind offer you can be off straight after lunch.'

Claire laughed. 'Put like that, how can I refuse? I intend to buy a little car for myself, but if it would give you pleasure to lend this to me until I buy one, it would give me pleasure to drive it.'

Claire arrived at the hospital a little before two o'clock. The hospital was quiet, settled into the lull that fell over most hospitals in the gap between lunch and visiting hours. Peggy came out of the office to greet her.

'Hi.' A big, welcoming smile was flashed at Claire. 'Alastair said you wouldn't be in today.'

'I'm a workaholic.' Claire smiled.

'You poor thing.' Peggy was all sympathy. 'It's not contagious, I hope?'

Claire shook her head, laughing. 'Where is everybody?'

'The patients are all supposed to be asleep, the rest of the staff are putting their feet up before the flowers start arriving and bells start ringing again, Rowena's off duty and Alastair's over at the clinic. Does that cover everyone?'

'Just about. How's Gil Francis?'

'Fine. He managed to pass the stone himself this morning and has been sitting up in bed bragging.

Alastair wants to keep him in for twenty-four hours just to make sure there was only one stone. Gil was complaining this morning about having to stay, but I just checked him a few minutes ago and he's sleeping like a baby. Although he wouldn't admit it, he's been badly frightened. He was still in a lot of pain when I came on duty this morning, and that was despite the pethidine.'

As Peggy spoke the phone started to ring in the office. She disappeared, leaving Claire with a list of patients and histories. Claire sat and started to read. She wasn't sure which of these people, if any, she could take responsibility for, but she hoped some wouldn't mind a female doctor.

Peggy returned looking worried.

'Trouble?' queried Claire.

'A problem,' the matron admitted. 'One of Alastair's elderly patients. He's got terminal cancer and Alastair's been looking after him at home. His wife thinks the end is pretty close now and wants Alastair to come. The problem is, Alastair's got twenty patients booked this afternoon.'

Claire looked at Peggy. She knew what was coming, and a little bubble of panic rose within her. Twenty patients in a totally strange environment!

'I suppose you could take over,' Peggy continued tentatively. 'Jean is a really competent receptionist. She could fill you in on all the administration details.'

'I suppose I could,' Claire said doubtfully. She caught herself and gave herself a mental shake. 'I mean, of course I could.'

'You can't.' Alastair's reaction to Peggy's proposal was blunt. 'For heaven's sake, this is your first full day in the country! You haven't a clue about the routine.'

'I've read everything I could get my hands on about general practice here,' Claire retorted. She looked firmly at him, deliberately blocking the memory of the night before. 'I need a pharmaceutical guide and help with official paperwork which I'm sure Jean can give me.' She nodded to an efficient lady surveying her with interest from behind the reception desk.

'I meant to spend a few hours with you tonight going over all the details.' Alastair ran his hand through his hair. Behind him, in the waiting-room, six pairs of eyes watched with interest. 'I'm way behind already. How do you think you'd cope?'

'I won't,' Claire answered softly. 'I don't know any histories and I'm unsure of the pharmacy list. I'll spend my time looking things up. By the time you get back I'll be further behind than if you'd stayed, but not as far behind as if you'd gone and I hadn't tried to take over. You do need to go, don't you?'

Alastair sighed. 'Yes. I've looked after Joe Conell since he was first diagnosed and I promised him and his wife I'd be there whenever they needed me. He was desperate not to come to hospital, and I'd hate to turn around and insist that he comes in at the end.'

'That's settled, then.' Claire flashed a smile at Jean. 'OK Jean, we're on our own.'

In the end it was easier than she'd imagined it could have been. Jean was a godsend. She had worked as the receptionist for the practice since before Alastair had started and knew every patient's background like the back of her hand. As she brought in each patient's history she outlined the probabilities for Claire.

'Mrs Thompson's next. She's coming to see you because her eyes have been bothering her again. She was telling me about it in the supermarket in Hamilton last week. Here's where Alastair keeps the equipment you'll need. If you think she'll need a referral there are two ophthalmologists in Hamilton—I've written their names and addresses down for you. Alastair prefers Dr Grandison, so suggest Dr Osmond. That way she's sure to want to go to Dr Grandison.'

Or, 'Betty Landman is here about her back. If I were you I'd do a bit of probing. Her daughter had a baby last week in Melbourne and I hear on the grapevine there's something wrong with it. I suspect Betty's back is just an excuse to come and talk to someone about the baby.'

Armed with such information, it was easy to ask the right questions, and Claire soon found herself relaxing and finding pleasure in meeting the stream of people coming through the surgery. Some of the patients were dismayed not to see Alastair, but the general reaction was curiosity, friendliness and, thought Claire, acceptance. She said as much to Jean as that lady declared a break and brought her a cup of tea.

'This town has been desperate for another doctor for a long time now,' Jean replied. 'The people are used to long waits. If you weren't here today they'd still be here tonight waiting to see Alastair, or would have given up and tried again tomorrow. The problem is there's been no guarantee that Alastair wouldn't be called out again tomorrow.'

'How on earth did he manage to get the time off to come to England?' Claire asked.

'It was a tough time,' Jean admitted. 'He persuaded a friend between jobs to act as a locum. Sam Cray didn't know what hit him. But Alastair had to go.'

'Why did he have to go?'

'Well. . .' the older woman's eyes rested on Claire '. . .you're here, aren't you?'

'You mean he went specifically to find a partner?' Again Claire felt the twist in her heart. How much had he tried to manipulate her? From the time of their initial meeting had he set out to pursue her with this in mind? She felt cold at the thought.

Jean shook her head as if sensing her thoughts. 'It wasn't entirely that. He had to do the obstetric course.' She paused, perched on the edge of Claire's desk.

'I guess you probably should know the reason.' She hesitated before continuing. 'We haven't been very well set up for obstetrics. Alastair's just been too busy. He's encouraged most of the local mums to deliver in Hamilton. Then about six months ago he was called to a dreadful road accident just out of town. There was a man trapped in the car and Alastair was away for about an hour. While he was away one of the local girls arrived here in the last stages of labour, and Peggy had to deliver her. The baby had all sorts of problems and there was nothing Alastair could do when he finally arrived. He said if he'd been here and had the right equipment and training he could have saved it. He was dreadfully upset. Anyway, he decided that night. He wanted obstetric training and a partner, and if he couldn't get them he wouldn't stay here.'

Claire gazed thoughtfully at her. 'Yes, well, one way or another I guess he's got them.' She put down her teacup. 'Who's next, Jean?'

By the time Alastair returned darkness was falling and the queue in the waiting-room was down to three. Claire was tired, but not as tired as Alastair. He must have been close to Joe Conell, Claire thought. He looked wrung out. He raised his eyebrows at the few people in the waiting-room and gave Claire a faint smile as she came out of the surgery with the patient she had just seen.

'Thanks, Claire. I'll take over now——'

Jean interrupted, 'Is Joe dead?'

'Yes—quite peacefully, about an hour ago. I see you're driving Mum's car, Claire. Do you want to go home? Mum'll have tea ready for you.'

'Dr Drummond, are you implying that Dr Bannon isn't competent to see the last few people?' Jean looked sternly at Alastair. 'Claire and I are managing very nicely, thank you, and you look about done in. Why don't you go over, do your rounds and talk one of the nurses into making you a cup of tea? That way you'll be ready to go home at about the same time as we are.'

Alastair threw a brief, questioning glance at Claire and at her answering nod he smiled. 'Thanks.' He turned to the three waiting patients. 'You don't mind seeing Dr Bannon, do you?'

'Get out of it!' An elderly man spoke up for the group. 'We've been waiting for hours to see the new lady doctor. You're not going to deprive us of it now.'

Alastair nodded tiredly and retreated.

'I hope you don't mind,' Jean whispered to Claire. 'Joe Conell was a friend of Alastair's dad. He'll be feeling it.'

'I don't mind,' Claire replied. 'I think I'm enjoying myself.'

Half an hour later she was finished. She bade her last patient goodnight, a young mother who had squeezed an appointment in at the last minute so her husbnad could be home to mind the children, left Jean doing the final clearing up and made her way over to the hospital. She felt tired but contented. The work was going to be within her capabilities, and the patients seemed to like her.

She found Alastair in the staff-room with Rowena. They looked up as she entered. Alastair's smile was faint but still there. He's had a bad time, Claire thought. Rowena didn't manage a smile. Her look was speculative and hard.

'All finished,' Claire threw at them, glancing almost defiantly at Rowena. 'I wasn't so slow after all.' She grinned ruefully at Alastair and added fairly, 'Thanks to Jean. She's worth rubies.'

'Isn't she just?' Alastair replied. 'She holds this place together.' He gestured to the teacups. 'Would you like a cup of tea?'

Claire shook her head. 'No, thanks. If it's all the same to you I'll get back to the farm. Dorothy said she'd have tea for me, and to be honest I'm looking forward to it.'

Rowena rose. 'I have to get back to work too. Are you staying for a while, Alastair?'

'Mm. Much as I'd love to go home, I'm still behind with the paperwork. Tell Mum I'll have something to eat here, Claire.'

'Fine.' Claire turned to go and discovered Rowena was following her.

She turned to Claire as soon as they were out of earshot of the staff-room. 'Tell Dorothy I'll slip out tomorrow with a couple of casseroles. She must be feeling the extra work. How long do you intend to stay out there?'

Claire drew in her breath. The barb was sharp and deliberate.

'For as long as Alastair and his mother make me welcome.'

Rowena gave her a hard look.

'Dorothy's not well. If you like we can put you up here. There is alternative accommodation to be found.'

'Why aren't you happy for me to stay at the farm?' Claire turned to face the other girl directly.

'Did I say I wasn't happy? Of course it's none of my business where you stay. It's just I feel a natural fondness for Dorothy and don't like to see her imposed on.'

Claire met the look for a long moment. Rowena wasn't even pretending to attempt friendship. Where did that leave Claire? Anger flickered within her and she suppressed it with an effort. She was looking for no enemies here.

'Goodnight, Rowena,' she said quietly. She turned her back on the hostile eyes and made her way to the car park.

CHAPTER SEVEN

Two weeks later Claire was beginning to feel as if she
had been at Gimboral for years. The work was stagger-
ing. From that first afternoon Claire had only to show
her nose at the hospital to find herself immersed in the
demands of a busy medical practice. Alastair didn't
spare her, acknowledging her desire to work hard, and
there was more than enough work for the two of them.

After Claire's first night in Australia, Alastair made
no attempt to approach her on a personal level. He's
got no reason to keep up the pretence now, she
thought, and the thought gave her a tiny pang. Their
professional relationship blossomed, however, as each
found they could work well together and complement
each other's skills.

Their normal working hours were spent in the clinic
with time out for a couple of surgery lists per week.
Claire took pleasure in the surgery. Alastair was
skilled, really more skilled than required by the type of
surgery he was normally called on to do. The major
surgery was sent to Hamilton or to Melbourne. Alastair
was at his best in emergencies, however. With long
distances to reach Hamilton or Melbourne, major
trauma had to be coped with at Gimboral. In a farming
community accidents seemed inevitable, and Claire
and Alastair found themselves constantly in theatre at
odd hours, setting fractures or trying to stabilise
seriously injured or ill patients before sending them on
to a bigger centre. With the demands made on her,

Claire was horrified to think how Alastair had coped alone.

'Raw strength and courage,' he grinned when she said as much to him. They were washing out a gravel rash. A local youth had come off his motorbike on a dirt track while wearing shorts and thongs. The gravel was so embedded Alastair had asked Claire to give a general anaesthetic while he cleaned it out. 'Being truthful, I didn't cope. I only did half a job. By the time I came to England I was acknowledging that I couldn't do the job on my own.' He laughed at her. 'Satisfied?'

'It's nice to be needed,' she said primly, her eyes not leaving the boy's face. It was minor surgery, but any general anaesthetic had to be painstakingly monitored. Claire often thought the surgeon had more free time than the anaesthetist during an operation. He at least could occasionally raise his eyes and see what was going on in the theatre.

Her patient was still a good colour. He was going to have few long-term effects from the accident, except perhaps a little scarring from the deeper lacerations. If he'd worn sensible clothes he wouldn't even have this damage, she thought.

'Silly young fool.' Alastair's words echoed her thoughts. 'He wears a helmet because it's illegal not to, but doesn't even think about the reasons we push for protective clothes on a bike. If he'd been travelling at a high speed this could have killed him. People don't survive without skin. There are good reasons for bikers to wear leather.' The nurse assisting handed him fresh solution and he bent over the job again. He scrubbed meticulously, using a firm brush and soapy aqueous chlorhexidine. A tiny amount of gravel left in the wound would mean it would take weeks longer to heal and would be much more likely to scar. As he scrubbed he separated and trimmed flaps of loose skin.

Finally the washing was complete. Claire prepared to reverse the anaesthetic as Alastair dressed the worst areas with vaseline gauze, dressing, pads and crêpe bandage. The minor areas were painted with mercurochrome. The boy was going to be a sight to behold for some time to come.

'All done.' Alastair stepped back and handed the last of the swabs to the nurse. 'Thanks, Claire. He wouldn't have been very happy to stay awake for that lot. Although,' he added reflectively, 'perhaps it would have made him think twice before he gets on a bike again wearing shorts.'

'I think he'll be sore enough to have learnt his lesson,' Claire replied. The boy's breathing resumed its natural rhythm, and she eased the tube from his mouth.

'Can I leave you to finish up here?' Alastair queried, casting an eye at the clock. 'I promised Mrs Conell I'd drop in on her tonight. She'll still thinking over Joe's death and rang to ask if I could see her and answer a few questions.'

'Sure.' Claire understood. Often it took a couple of weeks for the shock of a death to wear off, and a phase of the grieving process seemed to be the need to understand everything that went on at the end. 'I've a couple of patients of my own to see, so I'll be round until this boy is fully conscious.'

Alastair left. Claire finished up in the theatre and then did a ward round. There weren't many patients whom she could claim as her own, but there were enough to make her feel content. A few patients in the last week had actually asked to see her rather than

Alastair. She knew a lot of the reason was curiosity, but she hoped she was giving good service and they would be content to stay with her. She didn't intend to just look after Alastair's overflow forever.

When she finished she went back to the little room where the boy they had just treated was recovering. He was conscious, but disorientated from the effects of the anaesthetic and pain-killers. Claire left him as he drifted into a natural sleep.

His parents were waiting in the corridor. The police had contacted them and they arrived ashen-faced, fearing the worst. Claire reassured them and took them in to see their son. She left them sitting with him and went to find one of the kitchen staff to make them a cup of tea.

Finished at last, she cast a glance at her watch, and frowned. Dorothy would be waiting. Dorothy understood that fixed mealtimes were impossible for Alastair and Claire, but Claire was aware how much she looked forward to their coming home. With time hanging heavily on her hands all day it was no wonder. Claire grimaced to herself. Somehow there had to be some way she could help Dorothy. She stopped at the office to collect her belongings and made her way to the exit, still thinking of her friend. She was nearly at the door when Rowena burst in.

Rowena had been off for the afternoon and was wearing riding gear, tight-fitting white trousers, loose shirt and boots, with her hair casually caught back with a red scarf. She ignored Claire and made straight for the office, where Peggy was sorting through patient's files.

'Where's Alastair?'

Peggy looked up in surprise. 'He's on a house call, Rowena. Is there something wrong?'

'Whereabouts?' Rowena demanded.

Peggy shook her head. 'He didn't say. What's wrong?'

'Rory's hurt his foot. Damn fool, I told him Barcella wasn't ready for the wall, but he wouldn't listen. Barcella jibbed and shied, Rory came off and somehow Barcella stood on his foot. I'm pretty sure the ankle is broken. Are you sure you don't know where Alastair is? Didn't he take a history?'

Peggy's lips tightened at the accusing tone. 'Sister MacMillan, it is not my role to keep tabs on Dr Drummond when we have another competent doctor in the hospital.' She looked past Rowena at Claire, standing by the door. 'I'm sure Dr Bannon is more than qualified to deal with a broken ankle.'

Claire hesitated. Alastair had been trying to find time to see Mrs Conell for three days now. He was hardly likely to be happy being interrupted for something Claire could indeed handle.

'Of course,' she answered Peggy. 'Who's Rory?'

'He's my brother, and I'd prefer Alastair to see him,' Rowena said shortly. 'Where is he?'

Claire drew in her breath. Since her arrival Rowena had treated her with condescension bordering on contempt. The rest of the staff had seemed to accept her as a doctor, but she was left under few illusions as to what Rowena thought of her medical skills.

'He's at Mrs Conell's, but he doesn't want to be disturbed.' Claire met the girl's angry gaze calmly.

'I think he'll consider Rory more important than Mrs Conell,' snapped Rowena. 'Give me the phone book, Peggy.'

Claire drew in her breath, but before she could speak the door opened again.

Claire had no difficulty in recognising Rowena's brother. The resemblance between the two was clear. The MacMillans were a strikingly good-looking family, if Rowena and Rory were typical. Rory was much taller than Rowena. His slim build and muscular physique were accentuated by the riding clothes he wore with casual elegance. He stood holding on to the door, his face white beneath his tan.

'You said you were getting a wheelchair, Rowena.' His voice was petulant, edged with pain.

'Alastair's not here,' Rowena said tightly. 'I'm trying to find him.'

'And I'm to stay in the car until you do?' he queried unsteadily. 'Thanks very much!' He let go of the door and attempted to limp towards them.

The steps outside the hospital had rails beside them, and Claire realised he must have used them to support himself as he entered the hospital. Without any support his ankle gave. He gave a sharp exclamation of pain and would have fallen had Claire not moved. She caught his arm and he used it to right himself. He stood leaning heavily on her shoulder.

'Get a wheelchair, Rowena,' ordered Claire. Rory was no light weight and she could not support him for long. He was limp against her. If the ankle was broken it must have been an almost superhuman effort to climb those steps. She looked up at him. His eyes were almost closed, his head sagging. 'Rowena!'

Peggy saw the danger and moved before Rowena. She grabbed him from the other side, easing the intolerable weight. At last Rowena acted, seizing a trolley from beside the entrance. Acting in unison, the three girls lifted the almost inert man on to the prepared sheet.

'Take him into X-ray, Rowena,' Claire said. 'We'll have a look at the damage. Peggy, can you organise an injection of morphine for me, please? Fifteen ml intramuscularly.'

'I'd rather you didn't treat him,' Rowena repeated. 'Rory's a first-rate polo player, and his sport's important to him. I don't want him permanently incapacitated.'

'Neither do I,' Claire agreed softly, choosing to ignore the professional slur behind the words: 'If, after X-ray, it appears to be something I'm not capable of handling, then of course I won't treat him. I can certainly do no harm doing an initial assessment, though.'

'For heaven's sake!' The voice from the trolley was blurred but audible. 'You're a doctor, aren't you?' Rory's eyes had flickered open and he was watching Claire.

'I am,' Claire acknowledged.

'I'll choose my own doctor, thank you, Rowena. . .' The voice drifted and Claire had to lean to hear. 'You're it.'

The foot was badly damaged. It had obviously been crushed and was cut and bleeding. An X-ray revealed a non-displaced fracture, which meant at least that he didn't have to undergo surgery. Most of Rory's discomfort was going to come from the massive bruising.

Claire cleaned up the lacerations and inserted a couple of stitches. Peggy assisted while she applied a back plaster to hold the foot immobile, and Rowena watched silently.

'We'e going to have to put a full plaster on this

within a few days,' Claire told Rory, 'but it's not much use yet with this degree of swelling.' She grinned up at him. 'I'm afraid you're not going to be tempted to walk on it for a while anyway. You're in for a spell of enforced idleness.'

With the morphine taking hold, Rory had recovered his equanimity and was able to return the smile.

'There goes polo on Saturday, Rowena.' He was still smiling at Claire as he spoke.

'If you're finished,' Rowena addressed Claire through tight lips, ignoring Rory's last remark, 'I'll take him home.'

'Perhaps Claire would like me to stay here?' Rory looked calculatingly at his sister, then cast a long, speculative look at Claire. 'I could be convinced to stay.'

'You do what you damned well like,' Rowena snapped. 'I'm going home.'

Claire intervened. Rory MacMillan was not her idea of a perfect patient. She did not want conflict with Rowena, and she sensed that with Rory as her patient she would be exposed to the full blast of the girl's dislike. There was no reason to keep him in hospital. With relief she shook her head.

'Sorry, Rory, you don't qualify for a bed. I'll give you something to ease the pain over the next few hours and to help you sleep, but there's no reason why you can't do that in your own bed. Get someone to bring you in on Friday and I'll fit a full plaster.'

With relief she saw him settled in the back of Rowena's car. She and Peggy stood on the top step and watched them drive off.

'Why does Rowena distrust me so much?' she asked Peggy as they turned to go in. The question hung in the air between them. For a moment Claire thought Peggy wasn't going to answer it, but finally she looked sideways at her, seeming to make up her mind.

'It's not that she distrusts your medical skill, Claire. Alastair told us all that your training was first-rate, and your work here is bearing that out. You, however, are threatening Sister Rowena MacMillan, and she doesn't take kindly to threats.'

'Threatening? That's silly. How could I be threatening Rowena?'

Peggy cast Claire another sidelong look. 'If you don't know it's not for me to be telling you. Now if you want my advice you'll forget Rowena MacMillan and get off home and have some tea before something else happens.'

Claire went.

By the time Alastair arrived home Claire and Dorothy were soaking up the cool of the evening, drinking coffee on the back veranda. Claire was quiet, and Dorothy seemed to sense and respect her mood. As they finished their meal Claire attempted to stir herself and tell Dorothy about her day, and Dorothy listened in amusement as she heard about Rory's accident.

'Do him good to know what a little pain is,' she retorted unsympathetically. 'He's a grown man, but I often think in many ways he's still a spoiled little boy.'

'Mm,' murmured Claire non-committally.

Dorothy peered at her.

'You didn't like him?'

'He's very good-looking,' Claire countered. 'And he's got a lovely smile.'

'And doesn't he know it?' Dorothy said firmly. 'He's broken more hearts around here than I'd care to mention.' She took the tray on to her lap and started clearing dishes. 'Just make sure yours isn't one of them, Claire Bannon, or I'll wash my hands of you.'

'Fate worse than death!' Claire grinned. 'Don't worry, Dorothy. Personable young men of Rory MacMillan's ilk have more to concern themselves with than hard-working members of the medical profession——'

She broke off as Alastair appeared. Something had happened to irritate him. His face was creased into an expression of annoyance, and he gave his mother only a perfunctory kiss before sitting down and lapsing into silence. Dorothy gave a grimace across the table to Claire and then wheeled off with her tray of dishes. She was no sooner out of sight than Alastair began.

'Claire, I've just been across to the MacMillans' and learned what happened. Do you think it was right to insist on treating Rory yourself?'

Claire looked up questioningly. His face was stern and disapproving. A flicker of anger stirred within her.

'Do you think I'm incompetent as well?' she asked, trying to keep her voice calm.

'You know that's not what I think,' Alastair snapped. 'I wouldn't have asked you to come here if there was the least question of your competence. However, it shouldn't be so important to you to build up a practice that you insist on treating my friends when they've stated very clearly that they wanted to see me.'

'You were busy with Mrs Conell,' Claire retorted, stung by the injustice of his accusation. 'You know you didn't want to be disturbed.'

'Of course I didn't,' he said tiredly. 'However, when patients expressly wish to be treated by a particular doctor and are willing to wait, then I think we have to respect their wishes. You don't think you could have simply given Rory pain relief and left him for me to treat when I returned?'

'No,' Claire said firmly, 'I don't. There was not the least need for him to have to wait and, despite what Rowena may have told you, he was quite happy for me to proceed.'

'That's not what Rowena said.'

'Well, who do you believe?' She pushed back her chair angrily, grabbing the last remaining dishes on the table and pushed through the screen door into the kitchen.

Alastair stayed outside while Dorothy and Claire attacked the tea dishes. As they finished he appeared again, carrying a handful of glossy leaflets. He ignored Claire.

'Mum, I dropped in to Rowena's tonight to pick these up. It's all the information she offered to get on the retirement village at Warrnambool. Would you like to have a look at it now?'

Claire heard Dorothy's sharp intake of breath. She put down her dishcloth and quietly slipped from the room. Her presence wasn't needed.

She woke from a troubled sleep a couple of hours later. She lay listening in the dark until she was sure of what had woken her. Dorothy's room was next to hers, and through the wall came the sound of muffled sobbing. Claire rose and padded softly along the passage to Dorothy's door.

'Dorothy?'

Silence.

'Dorothy, can I come in?'

A bitten-back sob and then the sound of a nose being blown. Claire gently opened the door and crossed to the bed. Dorothy was a hump under the bedclothes.

'Are you under there?'

'No.'

'You're not crying either?'

'No, I'm not. I never cry.'

'Dorothy Drummond, that's a whopper!'

Dorothy emerged from the bedclothes and glared defiantly at Claire. By the light streaming in from the hall Claire could see her face was swollen and red with weeping. Hunched in the bed, she seemed absurdly small and frail.

'Well, wouldn't you?' she demanded. 'I'm being pushed into a retirement village and I don't even feel old. Useless, yes, but old, no. I've tried and tried to tell Alastair I don't want to go, but Rowena's made him believe I'm just saying that for his benefit. He really believes I'd be happier there, and I'm tired of arguing. I don't know what to say to him any more.'

'I'd tell him to go to blazes,' Claire said thoughtfully. 'Retirement villages are all very well for people who want to retire, but that's the last thing you want. Or is it?'

'I have retired.' Dorothy gave a watery sniff. 'I do nothing, and still they tell me I'm doing too much. What am I going to do in a retirement village? I won't even be able to knit for my grandchildren. Any grandchildren Rowena has any control over will be put in exclusive designer wear from birth, not my pathetic attempts at garments. I must admit,' she added truthfully, 'I probably wouldn't be seen dead in anything I had to knit myself.'

'Then you'd better not take up a knitting vocation,' Claire agreed. 'There must be other things.'

'Such as?' The elderly lady's voice was bitter.

'Well, like farming, for instance.' Claire took a deep breath. It wasn't any of her business, but the solution seemed obvious. 'Tell me, have you enough capital to restock your land?'

'Probably.' Dorothy eyed her dubiously. 'When we sold the cattle we invested the proceeds, and the leasing money from the MacMillans has been going into the same funds.'

'And how long is your lease with the MacMillans?'

'Twelve months mostly, but I insisted that the home paddocks were thirty-day. What on earth are you getting at?'

Claire stood up.

'Mrs Drummond, as your consulting physician I'm going to give you some advice. Tomorrow you give the MacMillans notice to withdraw—not completely, at least not all at once, just giving back as much as you think you could look after. When you get confident, perhaps you could take it all over again. It would give you an aim, something to work towards.'

'Oh, Claire, that's crazy!'

'Why? Are you as frail as everybody makes out or are you, as I suspect, as tough as old boots?'

'That's charming!' Dorothy's voice rose in indignation, and Claire grinned. The tears had gone out of Dorothy's tone.

'Well, someone's got to say it. I have a great respect for your son's medical knowledge, but I think in your case he can't see past the fact that you're his mother and he wants to protect you. I don't see you as a mother, or old or an invalid. All I see is a fit and able sixty-year-old who's growing old before her time. It's the worst service you can do for a patient, to treat them as an invalid after they stop being one.'

'Oh, Claire.'

'Don't "Oh, Claire" me. Just say, yes, Doctor, certainly, Doctor. As from tomorrow there are three career people living in this house; two doctors and a farmer.' Claire stopped and looked at the figure on the bed. 'Can you do it?'

Dorothy hesitated. She sat for a long time not saying a word, then looked up at Claire, her lined face slowly breaking into an uncertain smile.

'It's crazy.'

'No. It's certainly not going to be as easy as when you had your husband to help you, but I don't think it's impossible. I've been watching you these last few weeks, and you're not ready to be classified an invalid. All you're lacking is a useful pair of legs.'

'Would I have the courage?' queried Dorothy.

'I can't tell you that,' Claire replied. 'I guess it depends on how much you want it.'

'I'd have to have help.'

'Of course.' Claire felt a surge of hope at the interest in Dorothy's tone. 'You can't run a farm and do all Alastair's and my domestic chores. Between us all we need someone to help, and I'll gladly pay her wages.' Claire held up her hand to stop the interruption she could see coming. 'You won't let me pay rent, so this will be my contribution.'

Dorothy shook her head. 'There's heavy work I just couldn't do. I'd have to have someone helping on the farm.'

'Is that impossible to find?'

Dorothy's voice suddenly lifted in excitement.

'Davey Chandler'd come like a shot. He's a local lad who's a bit simple,' she explained. 'He's working in a sheltered workshop in Hamilton and hates it. I've always liked the lad, and I know if I had him to do the manual work we could manage.'

'And you could afford to pay him?'

Dorothy grew thoughtful. 'Yes.' Claire could see her mind stirring over all the possibilities.

'You'd need to be able to drive.'

Dorothy nodded. 'They tried to teach me at the rehabilitation hospital in Melbourne, but I wasn't interested. I reckon if I went down there for a week and learned, then bought myself a specially fitted little four-wheel-drive vehicle, I could bucket around this place like nobody's business.'

Claire laughed. 'I can see I don't need to keep making suggestions. If I'm not mistaken you've been thinking this through for a while.'

'Yes,' Dorothy admitted. 'It's just—well, when everyone else thinks you're frail it's hard to disagree with them.'

'Alastair will worry,' Claire agreed. 'You're his mother and he can't be dispassionate about you. He'll fret when you're "bucketing around" the farm, as you put it. It's up to you to convince him that you not only can do it but will enjoy doing it.'

'Help me, Claire?'

Claire smiled and bent to give the kindly face a kiss. 'I'll do my best. I'm not flavour of the month with your Alastair at the moment, but I'll try. Just don't let anyone talk you out of what you're able to do. Now, no more tears.'

'I told you,' the voice was indignant, 'I don't cry.'

'Neither you do,' Claire agreed, and went back to bed.

Claire left before the house was stirring the next morning. She had lain awake, restless and troubled, for most of the night, and the sound of the kookaburra's early morning laugh was almost a release. She had a mound of paperwork waiting at the surgery, so she made herself a quiet cup of tea and slipped out without disturbing the household.

She had worked steadily for nearly three hours and was nearing the end of the pile when Alastair flung open the surgery door and stood, his face rigid with fury. Claire looked up enquiringly.

'What the hell do you think you're playing at?'

'I'm sorry?' she queried.

'Don't play games with me!' Alastair strode into the room and stood towering above her. 'This stupid idea that you've put into Mum's head, that she can actually start the farm again. Have you got any idea how hard I've worked at the idea of her moving to this retirement village in Warrnambool? Last night she agreed. And this morning. . .' his voice grew mocking '. . .this morning she's been talking to clever little Dr Bannon who thinks she can solve all the problems of Gimboral after having been in the place for less than three weeks!'

'Perhaps it's because I've been here for such a short time that I can see things more clearly,' Claire said quietly. 'Your mother is very unhappy.'

'I know she's unhappy.' Alastair ran a hand wearily through his hair. 'She sits out there all day waiting for us to come home with no one to talk to. She's isolated and lonely.'

'And you think she'd be any less lonely surrounded by people she doesn't know, in a place she doesn't know?'

'There are thirty residents in the village, all around her age. How could she be lonely?'

'If I put you with thirty people with nothing in common except being roughly your age, are you sure you could make friends and be happy?' Claire asked. 'At least most residents of retirement villages have the desire to retire in common. Your mother hasn't even got that. She'd be desperately unhappy and spend her time trying to disguise it from you. She'd be moving to keep you happy, not for her benefit.'

Alastair looked at her for a long moment.

'You seem very sure?'

'I'm sure.'

'To keep me happy?'

'Yes.'

He slumped into the chair opposite her desk. Claire watched him with sympathy, her reaction to his anger easing as she thought of the responsibility he had been shouldering since the death of his father. He had tried to take the load from his mother. Now he was being told by both his mother and herself that his efforts had not been appreciated.

He looked tired and defeated. Watching him, she felt an unbidden wave of tenderness break over her. The urge to go to him and hold the bearded face to her breast was almost irresistible. She looked at the creases running from his eyes. If she held him she could smooth the worry away, ease his pain and assuage the ache within herself. In the silence she made a horrifying discovery. She was in love with this man—hopelessly, irrevocably in love.

He looked up and his gaze met hers. There was still anger deep within his eyes.

'What makes you so sure she can cope?'

'I'm not sure.' Claire fought to keep her voice calm and controlled. The emotion surging through her was bringing her close to tears. 'All I know is that she should be given the chance to try. You're so close to her that you don't see how fit she really is.'

'Rowena isn't as close as I, and she agrees. My mother is hardly fit to run the house, much less the farm.'

'Perhaps Rowena has another motive when she suggests retirement homes,' Claire said softly.

Alastair's head lifted. 'What the hell do you mean by that?' His voice was dangerously quiet.

She shook her head in dismay. She shouldn't have said it, but having uttered the words she now had to go on.

'I can't see Rowena sharing a house with your mother,' she said softly. 'I think if you're going to marry Rowena then you're going to have some difficult decisions to make.'

His expression hardened. 'Your imagination is playing some dangerous tricks, Claire Bannon. Of all the malicious statements. . .'

Claire rose. All she wanted to do was find herself a quiet cupboard and indulge in a bout of weeping, but she was going to stay calm, no matter what the cost.

'Maybe I'm wrong. I hope I am, but I don't think so. See how Rowena reacts when you tell her of your mother's change of heart. And now if you'll excuse me, it's nearly nine o'clock, and I have a ward round to do before morning surgery.'

He stood and looked down at her, the anger almost

palpable in the air between them. She met his gaze, desperately hiding the anguish she was feeling. This man was going to marry Rowena MacMillan. He could be no more to her than a colleague and a friend, and seemingly she had now destroyed the friendship. Colleagues only? What joy was there in that? She looked up at him, and sadness overwhelmed her.

Unbidden, tears sprang to her eyes. She felt them slip, warm and salty, down her cheeks. In dismay she lowered her gaze, fighting for self-control. This was dreadful! She was behaving like a teenager with a stupid crush. The silence stretched out interminably between them. Why didn't he go?

Suddenly his hand came out and caught her throat, forcing her to lift her face. For a long moment he stood staring into her brimming eyes, then with an oath he pulled her mouth up to meet his. His kiss was hard, brutal, punishing, and Claire could not respond or resist. She was confused, lost, out of her depth. Was this an act of anger and frustration, nothing more? It had to be. She felt her mouth, bruised and crushed under his. Unable to fight him, she submitted passively, waiting for the moment of anger to pass. Oh, God, to be loved by this man! What was she saying?

Then he was gone, and Claire was left staring at the closing door. She raised her hand to her bruised lips and sank back into her chair, the tears at last free to fall. She had hoped they could be friends. But with this between them perhaps they could not even stay as colleagues.

CHAPTER EIGHT

CLAIRE didn't discover what Rowena's reaction was to
Dorothy's decision. Whatever her true feelings, perhaps she'd had the sense to hide them from Alastair.
For the next few days Claire and Alastair exchanged
curt professional words, nothing more.

Peggy noticed the coolness between them and was
amused.

'You two had a tiff, then? Sister Anderson was
saying the atmosphere in Theatre this morning was
distinctly chilly.'

'Don't be silly,' Claire replied with a twinge of
discomfort. For heaven's sake, how many of the nursing staff had noticed?

Peggy grinned. 'Don't worry about it. The course of
true love isn't meant to be smooth.'

'Peggy——'

'OK, OK—I know when my comments aren't
wanted. Just take comfort from the fact that Sister
MacMillan is also going around looking like a thunder-
cloud. Now, about Mrs Kavanagh's medication. . .'

Claire responded to Mrs Kavanagh's medication
needs with relief.

A week previously Dorothy would have noticed the
tension between Claire and Alastair, but there was
now no time for sitting studying the moods of her son
or her guest. Within days Dorothy had lain such plans
that Claire was starting to wonder what she had set in
motion. There were lists from one end of the house to

the other. Stock reports, clearing sale notices, farming gazettes were piled on every chair. Alastair's first positive comment as he surveyed the mess was,

'Well, it's almost starting to look like home again.'

'He means he was brought up in a muddle,' Dorothy explained. 'I've always put the farm before housework.'

Her excitement was tangible, and in the face of it Alastair could not continue to be openly disapproving. He ceased to voice his doubts to Dorothy. With Claire, however, he maintained an icy indifference, and her unease deepened. This level of tension could not continue indefinitely. It seemed early to say that the job was not going to work out because they could not work out a professional relationship. Perhaps if she moved from the farm the situation would ease.

Rory arrived on Friday to have his back plaster removed and a full plaster applied. Claire was aware of a small surge of professional triumph when she learned that he had specifically booked for her to do the job. Rowena could now no longer keep up the fiction that Claire had treated him against his will.

By the end of his consultation, however, Claire's triumph had faded and she was beginning to think she would rather like to hand over this patient to Alastair. Rory MacMillan clearly thought he was the answer to every maiden's prayer, and she was having trouble keeping the consultation on a professional basis. Rory had obviously decided Claire was worthy of his interest. He was charming, personable and supremely confident. In the end she stopped being irritated and let herself be amused by his blatant conceit.

'What about coming to watch the polo tomorrow?' he demanded as she wrapped the wet bandages around his foot. 'It's on at our place, and we're running a dance afterwards. Come as my guest.'

'Well, you're going to be a lot of use as a partner at a dance, I must say,' Claire retorted. 'I'm not putting a heel on this plaster, and I don't want you weight bearing for a few days.'

'All the more time to sit and talk to you. Come on. You can't stay in this district and not get involved with its social life. You'll have the locals calling you a bluestocking, or worse, a snob.'

'Horror of horrors.' Claire grinned, and snipped the last of the rolls of dressing. 'There. Don't move for a while. I'll get Sister to bring you a cup of tea.'

'You haven't answered my question.' Rory reached out and caught her wrist, effectively stopping her from leaving the room. 'Will you come?'

Claire hesitated. It was true that she should get to know the local community, but she wasn't sure how much of it would be represented at the MacMillans'. From what she had seen, the polo set were likely to be drawn from throughout the state, their common factor being money rather than being of the Gimboral community. Still, maybe she was being unfair, judging polo players by Rory and Rowena alone. Perhaps it would be a good idea to have a night away from the farm and the tension there.

'All right,' she agreed with a smile. 'What time do you want me?'

'Two o'clock. I'd come to pick you up, but I suppose you won't let me drive either.'

'That's right,' she agreed imperturbably, reflecting inwardly that it was this very fact that made her agree to go. If it became unbearable, with her own transport she would be able to leave. 'Will I know anyone there?'

'I shouldn't think so. You haven't met my parents, and most of our friends travel quite a way for the match.'

'So the promise of meeting the community was just a ruse.'

He grinned, not in the least discomfited. 'Well, yes, but you've promised now, and there's no backing out.'

'Unless I'm needed here,' she reminded him. 'I don't know if Alastair has any plans for Saturday.'

'Oh, he's playing,' Rory said carelessly. 'Rowena persuaded him to stand in for me. He doesn't normally play, because of course he can't run to a string of polo ponies, but he's not a bad rider,' he added grudgingly. 'He's filled in for us before.'

'Then of course I can't come. You know one of us has to be on duty.'

'Nonsense. We've got the phone on and my mother doesn't watch, so she can relay any messages. If you're needed the hospital can contact you. Hey, Alastair!'

Alastair passed the surgery door and Rory hailed him as Claire still looked doubtful.

'Tell this obstinate woman she's allowed time off for frivolities tomorrow,' Rory demanded. 'She's partnering me at the dance.' His arm reached out and came around Claire's hips, pulling her close to him. 'You don't want her fading through overwork, do you?'

Alastair regarded them both with disdain.

'Dr Bannon is free to make her own decisions. And now, if you'll excuse me. . .'

Rory started after him. 'He's a pile of laughs. I can't think what Rowena sees in him. Never mind.' He turned back to Claire and pulled her tighter. 'Two tomorrow, then?'

Claire pulled herself away, embarrassed and angry. 'We'll see.' She stalked out of the door.

In the end she did go. The afternoon was quiet and hot. Claire did morning surgery and then faced the prospect of returning to the farm or sitting waiting for patients to come. She finished her paperwork for the week and then, out of excuses, she headed for the MacMillans'. She had never seen a game of polo and was interested despite herself. She tried to tell herself that Alastair's playing had no relevance, but she knew in her heart it was a lie.

It was slightly after two when she nosed the old Mercedes into the MacMillans' property. The polo match was not hard to find. The ground was surrounded by clusters of cars, most of them expensive makes and many with horse boxes on behind. From the centre of the ring of cars rose a cloud of dust. Cheering and the sound of horses' hoofs thundering on the hard turf broke the stillness of the countryside.

Rory had clearly been watching for her. He limped across on crutches as she pulled to a halt.

'Glad you could make it, Claire.' To her dismay he reached out, caught her and kissed her lightly, a proprietorial gesture that clearly stated his intentions for the day. He pulled her arm through his, showing considerable dexterity with the crutches, and made his way back to the group of spectators on the sidelines.

This was a far cry from the local get-togethers in the farming community where Claire had grown up. Claire had dressed casually in well-tailored trousers and a light blouse, her hair tied back with a gay scarf. Among these people, she acknowledged to herself, she felt underdressed and uncomfortable.

Not that they were formally dressed—indeed most of them wore riding clothes—but the effect achieved by the women was elegance and style. Liberty print scarves knotted under loose silk shirts, Dior or Gucci sunglasses pushed carelessly up on to superbly cut hairstyles, beautifully tailored riding breeches and boots that gleamed with expensive leather were the order of the day. Claire thought back to her pony-club days where the only prerequisites were a hard hat and wellingtons, and suppressed a smile.

The polo was interesting, and despite her discomfort with the surroundings she soon found herself drawn into the game. The pace was furious and she was wondering how the horses could take it. The heat was such that she found herself tired just standing in the sun, much less tearing around a polo field.

'They don't have to stand it for long,' Rory explained. 'The game is divided into chukkers. Each chukker is seven minutes long, and this is a six-chukker match. None of these ponies will be used for more than two chukkers, and those two not consecutively.'

'So that's why there are so many horse boxes?'

Rory nodded. 'With four players for each team, each needing at least three horses, there are a few horses necessary for the match.'

'No wonder it's an expensive game!' Claire exclaimed.

'Especially when you consider that each of these ponies is a thoroughbred and worth a mint,' he agreed. 'And then there's the time and cost involved in training them. It's not a poor man's sport.'

'No——' agreed Claire thoughtfully. She broke off as Alastair took possession of the ball and drove it skilfully through the goal. He played well, and the sight of him seated easily on the magnificent animal stirred her emotions. His breeches and loose shirt in the Gimboral colours accentuated the sheer maleness of him. His muscles showed as he changed position over and over, manoeuvring the horse to chase the wooden ball. He and the horse almost seemed as one, each seeming to anticipate the other's move. No wonder Rowena wanted him! If polo was her life, here was the perfect partner. Even if polo was not part of her life, Claire acknowledged with a surge of self-knowledge, Alastair could fill a girl's fantasies. With horror she suddenly realised where her imagination was taking her and gave herself a mental shake. This was Claire Bannon, who had devoted her life to medicine, thinking these outrageous thoughts. Resolutely she turned back to Rory and blocked out the sight of the dangerous picture of man and horse.

Rory's possessiveness was irritating. He used her as a support, lightly holding himself steady with an arm across her shoulders. As he performed introductions the grip tightened proprietorially, claiming her as his property among this crowd of strangers. During a break in the game Claire caught Alastair's eyes resting speculatively on the pair of them, and her colour rose. She lifted the hand away, only to be reproached by Rory.

'Do you want me to fall over, love? Have a heart!' The arm came back.

Just before the end of the game a messenger came across from the house. Claire was wanted at the hospital. She received the message with relief. She wasn't at home among these people and was increasingly aware of being regarded as a curiosity by Rory's friends. Another of Rory's women, she could sense them thinking, and she didn't like the categorisation.

'You'll be back here at eight tonight for the festivities?' Rory demanded as he saw her to her car.

'I don't know,' she replied truthfully. And then, not so truthfully, 'I'll come if I can.'

'If you're not here I'm coming to find out why—and there'd better be a good excuse,' Rory warned as she started the engine. He stood back and watched her as she revved the engine and manoeuvred the car around the horse boxes and back across the big, dusty paddock to the gate.

There was a baby waiting to be born back at the hospital, and Claire only just made it in time. Mr and Mrs Flattery's sixth child, and they greeted him with all the joy of a firstborn. There was little for Claire to do except join in the celebrations and help introduce five delighted little Flatterys to their new brother. She drove home humming. There was nothing like a straightforward delivery to make her feel at peace with the world. The MacMillans could have their polo set, she thought happily. There was no job like medicine.

Dorothy was locked in the study, no doubt wrestling with the intricacies of the requirements for the new fencing she had decided she must have. Claire ran herself a cool bath and lay soaking, trying to alleviate the oppressive heat. It was supposed to be autumn, she thought indignantly. March. Had someone forgotten to change the calendar? How long was this heat going to last?

She was roused from her musings by the telephone. Dorothy did not emerge. Some things were too important for interruption, and Claire grinned, remembering Dorothy's boredom of a week ago. She wrapped a big fleecy towel around her and padded into the hall.

'Claire? It's Peggy. We've got another one.'

'Another delivery? You've got to be joking!'

'Nope. It looks as if it's going to be soon too, so could you get a wriggle on?'

'Peggy, obstetrics are really Alastair's province. Are you sure this one is straightforward?'

'Just like the last,' Peggy reassured her. 'Fourth child. If you don't make it I'll deliver it myself.'

'I'll make it.' Two babies in one day! In Gimboral that amounted to a population explosion. Claire pulled on a fresh cotton dress and made her way back to the hospital.

She arrived just as the woman entered second stage and started to push. Mrs McKay was a big woman, in her late thirties. Her husband, clearly indulging in none of these new-fangled ideas of supporting his wife in labour, was out in the hospital garden gossiping to a couple of the nursing home residents. Clearly he thought there was no need to fuss. Claire scrubbed with speed. By the look of this all she had to do once again was catch.

The baby was born a couple of minutes afterwards, another fine little boy with a powerful set of lungs. Claire smiled down at the red little face creased in indignation at the bother he'd just been put to and handed him over to the sister. As she turned back to the mother things started to go wrong.

She glanced up at the face on the pillows, ready to congratulate her on her little boy. But her face was no longer ruddy with exhaustion, it was almost deathly pale. In alarm Claire looked down. Blood was oozing on to the sheet beneath her, quantities of blood, far too much for a normal delivery.

For a split second Claire froze in horror. A post-partum haemorrhage. The routine she had been taught was useless to her here—pick up the phone and call in a specialist obstetrician and the whole bevy of back-up available in a large city hospital.

Find the cause. Her mind flicked back into working gear and she did a fast examination. Nothing. The tear had to be high up. By the amount of blood it could be a ruptured uterus. She snapped an urgent message to the sister behind her as she administered another dose of ergometrine.

'Get Peggy!'

Where was Alastair? If it was a ruptured uterus he was her only hope. If they could operate fast, perhaps. . . She looked down at the bed and that hope died within her. The bleed was massive. She moved swiftly to take a blood-pressure reading. It was dropping while she watched. She looked up again at Mrs McKay's face. The woman was drifting towards unconsciousness.

Realising what was happening, the sister had left the baby in his prepared crib and moved swiftly to hit the panic button, three short rings on the bell. As Claire started a drip Peggy's face appeared at the door.

'Get Alastair!' snapped Claire. 'I need Theatre set up and I need blood, quickly.' Even as she said it she acknowledged the uselessness of it, but she had to try. Peggy took one look and disappeared. Claire turned back to Mrs McKay, searching for words to reassure her, but a glance was enough to tell her that the patient was no longer conscious. Claire gestured to the sister. The girl's eyes were wide with fright. 'I want pressure on the abdomen, now. I'll show you how.'

Once again her fingers probed for the source of the

bleeding, and this time she found it. Her heart contracted in horror. A massive rupture of the uterus. There was no way she could repair it without major surgery, and at this rate of loss there would be no time to even find the necessary equipment.

There was little she could do. While the sister applied pressure to try and stem the bleeding, Claire worked mechanically, trying to buy time. Peggy returned with blood, and Claire set the drip at maximum, then felt the pulse. It was faint and thready. She set up an oxygen mask and handed it over to Peggy to control.

'Did you find Alastair?'

Peggy shook her head, her eyes on the woman's face. 'They're trying to locate him now.'

Claire held the wrist. Fainter, fainter. She made an urgent gesture to Peggy, but the oxygen was already on full. She closed her eyes in defeat and the pulse was gone.

For a few moments there was silence in the theatre as the reality sank in. The sister was crying quietly, the tears flowing unchecked down her face. For perhaps three minutes nobody moved.

Peggy came out of her stupor first, mechanically starting to do what had to be done. Then Claire pulled off her blood-stained gown, picked up the little boy and walked out into the hospital garden.

'Mr McKay!' she called.

The man turned from the group of people he had been talking to and started eagerly towards her. As he neared her he suddenly slowed. Perhaps her face said it for her. Claire handed him the baby. He looked down at his son, then wonderingly up at her.

'Mr McKay, your wife is dead.'

*   *   *

By the time Claire had finished what had to be done at the hospital it was long past Rory's stipulated eight o'clock. She was exhausted, drained physically and emotionally. She finished the last of the paperwork and then went to find Peggy. Peggy was just going off duty. They looked at each other, their eyes reflecting the shock and horror of the day. At least Peggy's got her husband and five boys to go home to, thought Claire. She gave her a hug and it was returned fiercely—most unprofessional but necessary.

'Now, don't you go dwelling on it,' scolded Peggy, surveying Claire with a worried look. 'You know you did your best, and no one in the same circumstances could have done better. I've never seen anything like that in my entire nursing career, and I bet neither have you. Some things you can't fight, and when that happens you've just got to accept them and go on.'

'Yes, Mum.' Claire smiled wanly.

Peggy returned the smile and gave her another quick hug. 'I've got to go—I promised I'd drive Sister Ray home. She's feeling as sick about this as we are.' She pulled on her cape and started towards the door. As she pulled it open she turned to Claire. 'Go home and get some sleep.'

Claire nodded, but she knew there was going to be little sleep for her that night. After telling the sister-in-charge where she was going she made her way out to the hospital garden. What she really needed was a good long walk, but Alastair was still at the MacMillans'. Peggy had phoned to cancel the message that he was needed at the hospital. He at least could still have a carefree night, although it meant that Claire was still on duty. She sat down on the lawn, her knees hunched up under her chin, and let the silence seep into her. The only sound was the strident chirping of the crickets, buried deep beneath the lawn.

Alastair found her there an hour later. She was aware of the door of the hospital opening, and his figure silhouetted against the light while he searched for her. When he saw her he pulled the door shut and crossed the grass to crouch beside her.

He didn't say anything, just knelt and watched her in the dim light thrown out from the hospital windows. Claire tried to meet his gaze, but failed. Her body was doing strange things. She was shivering uncontrollably, although the night was still and hot. She felt as if she wanted to cry, but the tears wouldn't come.

Alastair placed a finger under her chin and raised her face so he could see it. Still Claire could not meet his gaze. If only she could control the tremors sweeping over her body in sickening waves! He moved until he was kneeling on the grass in front of her, then gently put his arms around her and drew her into him.

She resisted him, keeping her body rigid against him. He didn't fight her, just moved a hand up to stroke her hair. He waited, the silence, the tension and the events of the afternoon building up to a crescendo within her. Suddenly it was too much. Tears started coursing down her face, and with the tears came release. The slow stroking continued, while Claire buried her face into Alastair's shoulder and wept as she hadn't wept for years.

How long they stayed like that she couldn't tell. The awful shivering stopped and the shuddering sobs gave way to a blessed calm. She stayed encircled within his arms, drawing warmth and strength from his body. Slowly the lingering horror faded and a measure of acceptance and peace took its place. Still she made no move to break away. Here was a haven, here was her love. She acknowledged it to herself almost unconsciously.

Alastair was the first to break the stillness.

'Why did you cancel the message to me? I still would have come.'

'There was no point. There was nothing for you to do.'

'Except to support you.'

'I could cope on my own.'

He shook his head. 'Counselling grieving families when you're still in a state of shock yourself is a grim task. I could have spared you that.'

'How did you find out?' Claire looked up wonderingly at him. He was still loosely holding her, his arms around her waist.

'Peggy dropped in to the party on the way home. She was worried about you.'

'She shouldn't have. I'm fine.' She gritted her teeth and continued, 'If it had been at St Mark's we might have saved her.'

Again Alastair shook his head. 'That's highly unlikely. Peggy said you hardly had time to get a drip up.'

'But if we'd had theatres set up and a team of doctors——'

He held up his hand. 'OK—I concede that with four doctors and all the facilities available at ten seconds' notice she might have made it. Is that going to make you feel guilty?'

'It's just. . . Should we be practicing here, where we haven't got the facilities?'

'Someone has to.'

'Do they? If we weren't here wouldn't the women go to one of the big centres?'

'No.' Alastair's voice was firm. 'That's one of the reasons it's so damn hard to attract doctors to country centres. They can't handle the responsibility of not having specialist back-up and feel guilty when things go wrong. What they don't realise is that worse things happen when they're not here. If Margaret McKay didn't have this hospital to come to she would have been faced with spending four weeks before the baby's due date kicking her heels in the city waiting for it to be born. With three other children it would have been prohibitively expensive and impractical. She would have elected to have the baby at home.'

'With the same outcome,' Claire said bitterly.

'With the same outcome,' Alastair agreed. 'But most birth complications, thank heaven, aren't as calamitous as a ruptured uterus. I've never had that happen, and I've seen a lot of babies born. Most things we can help with—breech births, long labours, flat babies. We can deal with them much more efficiently than the women could at home without medical care, and for most farming women I believe that's the option. Now,' he pulled her to her feet, still holding her casually against him, 'enough soul-searching. I'm taking you home.'

Claire rose slowly. She felt numb and lifeless, as if all the vitality had been sucked from her body. Alastair held her still, and she leaned heavily against him. Her leg ached dully. Somehow she had to find the energy to leave, to go back to the farm and get to bed.

'I'm fine.' She made a token effort to pull away. 'I don't need you to take me home. Go back to the party.'

'I've lost my party spirit,' he said grimly. 'Don't

forget, Margaret McKay has been my patient for a long time.'

'I'm sorry,' she said contritely. 'It's another thing I'm not used to. In the country everyone's involved when something like this happens.'

'Donne's "Any man's death diminishes me," holds doubly true in a small country town,' Alastair agreed gravely. He took her hand and turned towards the entrance. The door opened and a shaft of light swung out at them. Rowena appeared in the doorway.

'There you are!' Her voice was tinged with annoyance and suspicion. She ignored Claire and addressed herself to Alastair. 'Rory said you came back here to help Claire, but I thought he must have been mistaken, when I saw the hospital was so quiet. Did she need help?' Her tone was laced with sarcasm.

Alastair's hand tightened on Claire's.

'Mrs McKay died in childbirth, Rowena. I came back to see if Claire needed some support.'

'Oh.' For a moment Rowena floundered, then recovered her equilibrium. 'How dreadful for you, Claire. Of course you must be distraught.' She said it easily, her expression moulding to one of concern. Claire fought back a sudden urge to slap her lovely face.

'I'm fine,' she said tightly. She pulled away from Alastair's hand. 'It's time I was home, though, if you'll both excuse me.'

'You're not coming back to the party?' Rowena asked in surprise. 'Rory's livid. He's been ringing here every half hour and they've been saying you were unavailable.'

As Claire had instructed them to do. She could do without Rory tonight. He would have to make do with someone else. He didn't strike Claire as being a young man who would pine alone for long. She shook her head with weariness; she was too tired to argue.

'Claire, I'm driving you home,' Alastair repeated.

'We can drop you off on our way back to the party,' Rowena agreed pleasantly. 'I had one of the people leaving early drop me here,' she explained to Alastair. 'I knew you'd take me back.' She tucked her arm possessively through his.

He gave a grimace of annoyance. 'Rowena, I'm not coming back——'

'It's all right,' Claire broke in, 'I've got your mother's car and I'm fine to drive. You two sort yourselves out. I'm taking myself home. I would appreciate it if you could take any calls tonight, though, Alastair.' She left them and made her way out to the car, fighting an absurd impulse to dissolve again into tears.

Claire lay awake in the big bed, watching the flickering patterns made by the fan whirring gently in the soft moonlight. Sleep eluded her. She had been home for hours, tired beyond belief but so pent-up with conflicting emotions that her active mind would not give her body the sleep it craved. She went over and over the events of the afternoon. Was there anything else she could have done? Of course there wasn't. Why not let it rest, stop thinking about it?

What was Alastair doing at the moment? Her mind flicked back to the polo match, and the image of him seated astride the thoroughbred pony pervaded the night. She stirred uneasily in the bed. She remembered her first impressions of Alastair Drummond, seemingly an age and half a world ago. She had thought he was dangerous, and so he was. Her heart was no longer her own.

She would have to get away from here. How could she stay working, feeling like this?

Perhaps it would be better if she left. Country medical practice was demanding in the way that city medicine could never be. In the city there were people to hand over responsibility to. Claire didn't feel old enough or qualified enough for the responsibility now resting on her shoulders. Alastair had said there was no one else willing to shoulder that responsibility. Well, why should she feel guilty at leaving? She wasn't even Australian, for heaven's sake! 'Come and give it a try,' Alastair had said. Well, she had given it a try, and she didn't like what she saw. The only thing to decide now was whether to try out a job in Melbourne or Sydney or to simply go home.

She resolutely turned her shoulder to the wall. Instead of making her feel better her decision had left her cold and desolate.

'Claire?'

It was a whisper, no more, echoing around the big, moon-filled bedroom. Claire drew in her breath.

'Are you still awake?'

She bit her lip. She lay still, her eyes wide, staring into the dark. Surely he would not come in. As she watched the door opened slowly and Alastair came into the room.

She shut her eyes in panic, feigning sleep. Dear heaven, this man did such things to her!

She felt rather than saw him approach the bed. He stood for a long-drawn-out moment, watching her. Very gently he traced the outline of her face, running his finger down her cheek with a feather-light touch.

'Goodnight, Claire.' In the stillness she could only just hear him. He bent over and his lips softly brushed her brow.

Her eyes flew open. His breath was warm on her face. The deep shadow of his face towered over her.

She knew she should recoil in disgust, order him out of her bedroom, away from her. Cold reason fought in her head, screamed at her not to be stupid. Cold reason lost. Her arms came from under the sheet and twined themselves around the dear head, pulling the dark shadow down to merge with her.

It was as if it were happening in a dream, a warm, lovely dream where all things were possible. She drew him downwards, and Alastair sank slowly on to his knees. His mouth found hers, and they melted into each other, each responding with a fierce, almost desperate hunger.

Claire had never known she could feel like this. Her whole body was alight, surging with love and desire. This man was the only thing that mattered. For now he was hers. Nothing else was important. They drank their fill, their tongues moving from mouth to mouth, intertwined, locked, one.

Alastair was the first to break away. He pulled back, enough to look at her in the filtering light.

'Claire.' His voice was hoarse with passion. 'I didn't mean. . .'

Claire laid a finger on his lips. 'Hush.' She ran her fingers through his hair, tracing the contours of his head. 'Hush.'

'My heart, are you sure?'

She closed her eyes, letting the exquisite sweetness of the moment soak in.

'For tonight,' she whispered, tracing the outline of his lips with her fingers, 'for tonight, all I want is you.'

With a groan he sank down beside her. Her mouth was taken into his again and she was lost, drowning in waves of pleasure.

His hands slowly moved over her, tracing the outline of her body under the flimsy nightgown. He held her hard, pulling her breasts against him, then her waist, then around to pull her firm buttocks hard against him. The hands rose again, around to slide underneath the lacy cotton to feel the firm rise of breasts beneath.

As their need for closeness grew they rose, each driven by the same desire. Alastair pulled the wispy cotton garment up and over her head. As her arms rose his mouth dropped to the proudly upright nipples, taking each by turn, caressing, teasing and tantalising until Claire was on fire, her body screaming with her need. She fell back on to the sheets, willing him to follow.

'You have to wait,' he whispered softly, leaning forward to run a finger down through the deep cleft between her breasts, across the flatness of her belly and then lightly down between her open legs. 'No babies tonight. Not yet.' His voice held amusement, tenderness—love? 'Wait, my love.' Then he was gone, leaving Claire to lie suspended, bound by an aura of the inevitable. This was right.

At last he was back, standing above her, his eyes possessing her silk-smooth body. She lay savouring the moment as he rid himself of his clothes. As she watched him in the moon's soft rays she marvelled at his hard, muscled body, aching to feel his skin on hers. The last garment fell away, and her eyes widened at the look of him. She reached out to feel the fine hairs on his stomach.

There was no trace of hesitation or shyness. This man was hers. She pushed herself up and lightly kissed the flatness of his belly, and he let out a long sigh of pleasure. 'Wait just a moment,' he commanded, then, 'My love,' he whispered, as he lowered himself on to the bed. Gently, languorously, he lay until their skin met for the full length of their bodies. A tremor of exquisite anticipation ran through Claire. Feeling it, Alastair pulled back in the half-light, searching the shadow of her face. Reaching down, he gathered her up in his arms, cradling her, rocking her body against his. Claire turned into him, raising her face to his, sliding her arms around the smooth hardness of his back. Skin against skin, warmth against warmth. Let tomorrow bring what it would; tonight there was only her need of him. She lifted her hand and stroked the hair back from his brow, then pulled his face down to kiss each eyelid in turn.

His control broke. He gave a low moan and thrust her back across the bed. She pulled him back down to her, guiding him, melting her body into his. She arched her body up into his and felt at last the perfect pain, the rightness of his body entering hers. Then, as the joy became an unbearable longing, the fever of passion took hold, sending wave after wave of almost unbearable sensation. They clung and moved in a perfect rhythm, and when the peak came they reached it together, a shattering, tumultuous joy that left Claire wondering whether life could ever be the same again.

CHAPTER NINE

CLAIRE'S first reaction as she surfaced into early morning consciousness was of pleasure, pure sensual pleasure. Her body felt warm and sated, like a baby who has drunk his fill from a beloved breast. She stirred languorously in the bed and opened her eyes. Suddenly remembrance flooded back and the pleasure evaporated as if it had never been. She looked across at the hollow moulded into the pillow beside her. He was gone.

What had she done? With a moan of despair she buried her face in the covers. She shook her head back and forth in disbelief. It had not been her, Claire Bannon, welcoming Alastair into her bed. It was a person she had never met before, a creature she had no control over. Heat flooded into her face. What had he thought of her?

He had called her 'my love', 'my heart', she remembered, and the awful cringing eased. Perhaps he meant it. If she were truly loved. . .

Don't be stupid, she told herself firmly. He came in to see if I was still upset and I threw myself at him. What man could resist that? She closed her eyes hopelessly, silent tears squeezing between the lids. She turned into the pillow and let her unhappiness take its course.

She rose late, ran herself a bath and lay soaking in the cool water. She needed to pull herself together, to come to some sort of decision before she faced the world. In the end she did. Lying in the quiet, she knew there was only one course of action open to her.

She told Dorothy first. How much that lady had heard from the next-door bedroom the night before Claire had no way of knowing. Apart from a sharp glance at Claire's swollen face, however, she made no comment and sat chatting about the weather as Claire ate her breakfast.

'It's going to hit the century today, or I'm a Dutchman,' she remarked.

'A century?' Claire shook her head in confusion.

'The temperature,' Dorothy explained patiently. 'Oh, for heaven's sake, do you have that awful Celsius business in England? We have it here too, so I'm told, but I won't have a bar of it. Who wants to know whether we've reached thirty-eight point seven or whatever? When it reaches a hundred, I'm hot!'

Claire attempted a smile, stirring her coffee reflectively. It really was hot. She could feel beads of perspiration starting at the back of her neck.

'When are we due for autumn?' she enquired.

'Soon, I hope,' replied Dorothy with a worried look. 'This place is a dust-bowl. If a fire came through now we'd be in real trouble.' She turned her gaze to the window and her frown deepened. The harsh north wind was blasting dust and debris up on to the veranda, scorching the side of the house. It was early yet, Claire reflected. By afternoon, it was going to be unbearable.

'You wait till you see this place after the autumn rains,' Dorothy mused. 'You won't recognise it for the same place. A touch of green and Ardlethan is lovely. Especially,' she added ferociously, 'when I get rid of some of those damn sheep and put my beautiful Herefords back in their place.'

Claire placed her cup carefully back in its saucer.

'Dorothy, I won't be here to see it. I'm sorry, but it's not working out. I'm going home.'

For a long moment there was silence, Dorothy's eyes on the unhappy ones before her. Finally she spoke.

'Back to England?'

'I think so. I'm going to check out the job situation in Melbourne and Sydney, but really,' and as she said it the truth of it hit her with force, 'I think I just want to go home.'

'Because of what happened yesterday?'

'In part,' Claire agreed.

'And because you're in love with my son?'

Claire's eyes flew up and met the kindly green ones. She couldn't say anything. For a moment there was silence, then Dorothy's hand came out to cover hers.

'My dear, you don't have to agree or disagree. It's none of my business. I just wish. . .Well, it doesn't make any difference what I wish.'

Claire toyed with her spoon, then in sudden decision forced herself to ask the question that had been occupying her mind almost solely from the moment she woke up. 'He is going to marry Rowena, isn't he?'

Dorothy shook her head miserably. 'I don't know. I suppose so. Certainly it's what Rowena has been telling him and me and the whole district since they were children.'

'You mean it's been all her idea?'

'No.' Dorothy shook her head. 'I'd like to agree, but it's not fair. I think Alastair proposed quite seriously to the only decent-looking twelve-year-old in the district, and he and Rowena have been considered a couple ever since.'

'And does he love her?'

'Who knows?' Dorothy asked bitterly. 'I'm only his mother.'

Claire didn't see Alastair until later that morning. She had done a slow ward round, spending a lot of time with each patient. The hospital was unnaturally quiet, even for a Sunday, with shock rebounding through the small community at the news of the death the day before. There was no sign of Alastair.

Claire entered the nursery feeling oppressed. The newest Flattery was with his mother, but little Jamie McKay was there for her to see. At the entrance the sister-in-charge beckoned her and gestured into the room.

'There's someone here to see you. She's been here all morning. Dr Drummond said it was OK if she waited in here.'

As Claire entered a woman rose from a chair beside Jamie's crib. She came towards Claire and held out her hand.

'You must be Dr Bannon. I'm Enid McKay, this wee one's auntie.' She took a deep breath, as if she had been practising in her mind what she wanted to say.

'I just want you to know that this little one's going to be fine. They all will be.' She nodded her head decisively. 'Marg and me were as close as sisters, even though we were only sisters-in-law. My Harry was killed when we were engaged and there's never been anyone else. I've been treated almost as one of their family ever since.' She paused for breath, obviously finding the going difficult, but went on determinedly.

'I know what you went through yesterday—Doc Drummond told us this morning. I just want you to know that the kids will still have a mum, at least as close to one as they can get without the real thing.' A tear rolled down her cheek and she wiped it away impatiently. 'And I know you did your best yesterday. That's all any of us can ask.'

'Thank you,' Claire said gently.

'No,' the woman looked away, trying to hide her emotion, 'it's us who thank you,' she said gruffly.

Dangerously close to tears herself, Claire checked the baby and left him to the care of his aunt. At least one worry had been lightened. There was a lot to be said for extended families. With her mind deep in thought she didn't look up as she walked out of the room. Suddenly Alastair was right in front of her.

With an exclamation she drew back, her face turning a deep crimson. She backed against the corridor and stood, speechless.

'Claire. . .'

He held out a hand to her, but she warded him off with a gesture of denial.

'Don't.' She forced herself to speak.

'Claire, I'm sorry.'

'Don't be sorry.' It was almost a cry of pain. 'Don't be sorry.'

'Claire. . .' Alastair seemed almost as much at a loss as she. 'Claire, come outside. We need to talk.'

'We don't need to talk,' she forced out. 'I'm leaving here, Alastair. I've patients booked until the end of this week. I'd like to say I'll stay until you find someone else, but that could take months. I'm leaving on Friday.' She turned and walked away, leaving him staring down the corridor after her.

She didn't go back to the farm. Any company, no matter how sympathetic, was oppressive to her today. Alastair was on call and she needed to be alone. The

heat was intense, a searing, scorching heat that pervaded every crevice. Five minutes outside was more
than Claire felt she could stand. She thought longingly
of the coast. Thirty kilometres, Alastair had said, and
the big old car was not air-conditioned. She didn't
think she'd make it. She stifled a feeling of claustro-
phobia. There had to be somewhere she could go.

Finally she thought of the river. River? The label
was a joke, but it would have to do. She climbed into
the hot car and nosed her way down to the bridge.
Local children of all ages were whooping and splashing
in the swimming hole. Leaving them to their fun, she
drove out of the town, following the course of the river
as closely as she could.

She drove for perhaps three kilometres before the
river finally came back to run near the road. Here it
broadened slightly. The water was shallow but still
running, with a couple of huge river red gums providing
a massive leafy canopy over the water. The road Claire
was on was little more than a track. She parked the car
and climbed out. With luck she could have a couple of
hours' solitude.

She had a book with her in the car and for a while
she tried to read, seated on a cushion of loose twigs
and leaves with her back against a vast tree-trunk. It
would be nice to have some soft grass to sit on, she
thought, and her mind turned to home. Yorkshire in
March—cold, bleak. Though there would be grass
there wouldn't be much fun being in the open. This
place was bleak too, but in a different way.

She threw the book aside impatiently. The water
beckoned her, and she abandoned her sandals and dug
her toes into the current. The river, at its deepest, was
up to her ankles. Probably just as well, she thought.

The urge for a swim was almost unbearable. If the water had been deep enough she would surely have disregarded her lack of swim-suit and taken the plunge.

She paddled slowly downstream, trying to find some peace within herself. There was none. She was a mass of conflicting emotions, all crying out to be heard. In the end she came to only one decision. She would not work in Sydney or Melbourne. If Alastair Drummond had brought her to the state of a fluttering schoolgirl who only had to see him to forget every resolution she had ever made then she had to get as far from Alastair Drummond as possible. She was going home.

And then what? The future stared bleakly before her. If only I hadn't let last night happen, she thought. I never need have known how good it could be. She bit her lip and kicked a spray of water out in front of her. As she did so her toe came in contact with a stone. The pain was almost welcome, a release from the deeper pain within. She returned to the bank and her leafy mound. It was too uncomfortable to sleep, even if sleep were possible for her tangled mind. Finally she simply sat, watching the patterns the hot wind made on the water until finally the slight letting up of the heat and the lowering of the sun signified the day's end.

She was hungry, hot and tired as she drove the few kilometres back to the farm. All she wanted was a bath, a salad and bed. She parked the Mercedes and walked slowly around to the entrance. Alastair was waiting for her on the veranda.

'Did you have a good day?' His tone was one of polite enquiry.

'Yes, thank you.' She made to brush past him, but he rose swiftly from the big canvas chair and caught her arm.

'Claire, we need to talk.'

'Why?' Her voice was lifeless, flat.

'Because I want to marry you.'

She stopped pulling from his grasp and turned back to him. Her eyes widened in amazement.

'Claire. . .' He paused and ran a hand through his hair, obviously at a loss. He looked at her in desperation, willing her to help, but Claire was silent. She could not believe what she was hearing.

'Hell!' He reached out for her hands and she allowed him to take them. She stood passive, waiting. Only as he tried to pull her closer did she resist. He abandoned the attempt and stayed holding her hands in his, looking down into her dark-ringed eyes.

'Claire, can I make one thing quite clear? I am not now, nor have I ever been, engaged to Rowena MacMillan. Rowena has been my friend. She's helped enormously when I've been in trouble, but I don't want to marry her. The only woman I want to marry is you.'

'You didn't tell me that last night.' Claire's voice was almost a whisper, laced with pain.

'I didn't think I had to,' he exploded. 'God, what we had together! What we have together! Claire, you must feel it too. I didn't think I needed to stop and promise you marriage.'

'No,' she agreed. She felt as if she were speaking from a long way away. Her voice didn't seem her own. 'I didn't ask for any promises and I'm not asking for any now.' She bit her lip and glanced up at him, then sharply away. 'Alastair, I know how much you need a doctor here, but I can't stay. I can't. Not even if you make the supreme sacrifice and marry me to keep me here. All you've done with that offer is to make it more necessary that I leave.'

Finding courage, she looked up at him, anger joining the conflict of emotions within her. 'Next time you find a potential partner I suggest you be honest with them from the start.' She broke on a sob and pulled at her arms, but Alastair's grip deepened.

'You still think that's why I made love to you?'

'Well, what else can I think? You've got your beautiful Rowena. Is she to be sacrificed so that Gimboral gets another doctor? Does she think it's worth it? Why else would you want me? I'm a cripple, don't you remember? Ask Rowena, if you've forgotten—she'll tell you. The doctor who had to come here because no one else wanted her!'

'Claire, this is crazy!'

'Is it?' She was past caring what she said now. Tears were sliding down her cheeks, but her overriding emotion was fury. 'Is it?' She pulled hard back on her hands and broke from his grasp. 'Isn't that the way you'll remember me? Claire Bannon, emotionally and physically damaged. It'll be a balm to your pride. I won't marry you, Alastair Drummond.' She choked on a sob. 'And I pity the lady who does, even if it is Rowena MacMillan!'

She turned and fled into the sanctuary of her bedroom. She slammed the door and looked down at the lock. There was a key protruding. She turned the key and slipped it into her pocket before sinking on to her bed. There must be no repetitions of last night for the five nights she had left to her at Gimboral.

Claire emerged on Monday morning pale but resolute. She had a busy week booked. If she was only to stay another week at least she would give value for service while she was here.

It was just after six a.m. as she entered the kitchen, but Dorothy was still before her.

'Don't you ever sleep?' Claire demanded.

'In winter,' Dorothy retorted. 'Who can sleep in this heat?' She motioned behind her to the short-wave radio. 'I've been listening in to the CFA.'

'CFA?' queried Claire.

'Country Fire Authority,' Dorothy explained patiently. 'There's outbreaks of bush and grass fires all over the state. Nothing near here yet, though, touch wood. These are the worst conditions I've seen for years.'

'Is Alastair up?'

'He's gone.' Dorothy cast a quick glance at Claire, then looked away. 'I don't think he's sleeping very well either.'

'Who can in this heat?' Claire crossed to the window and looked out. 'This is awful. I think I'll almost be grateful for a bit of English winter.'

'You're not giving this place a chance,' Dorothy retorted. 'Fancy coming to Australia in February and going home in March! You'll spend the rest of your life thinking this country is a hot, windy dust-bowl.'

'And so it is,' Claire retorted. She didn't add that that was the image she wanted to take home. She wanted no fond memories to haunt her.

As she left she stopped at the screen door and looked worriedly back at Dorothy.

'Dorothy, are you going to be all right here by yourself?' She held up a hand to ward off the expected indignant response. 'I mean, what if a fire did come through? What would you do?'

'Yell for help,' Dorothy assured her. She motioned to the radio. 'That's why I've got that. Even if the phone lines are out I can still contact the fire boys, plus every farm that's got a receiver. Most of them have here.'

'Why not come in with us and spend the day in the hospital garden?' Claire suggested worriedly.

'And join the other old dears with their knitting?' Dorothy demanded. 'No, thank you, dear. I've already told you what I think of that.' She smiled up at Claire. 'Don't fret, child. I've trained Alastair not to. Don't you start.'

Claire smiled and reached down to give her a hug. She left, her mind not totally reassured but aware that short of forcibly dragging Dorothy into the car with her there was little she could do. Dorothy had booked in to a training course to learn how to drive a specially equipped car in a fortnight. Claire could only wish she had those skills now.

As she reached the hospital Dorothy's situation eased into the back of her mind as the day's work took over. People thought winter was the great killer, she reflected, but a summer like this took a worse toll. The surgery was full of people with breathing problems caused by the dry, dust-filled air. Every minor gastro-enteritis became a major problem as the combination of the heat and the illness caused dehydration. The children's ward filled as Alastair and Claire set up intravenous drips to restore depleted fluids and set up oxygen tents for the little asthmatics. Claire worked solidly, wondering as she did so how on earth Alastair was ever going to manage alone. It's not my problem, she told herself firmly.

Halfway through the afternoon she was called out of the clinic urgently. She made her way over to the hospital to find Peggy and Rowena attempting to extricate an elderly woman from the passenger seat of a car parked at the hospital entrance. As Claire reached them they succeeded in lifting the woman on to a trolley and wheeled her in the hospital entrance. A man of similar age followed the trolley in, obviously beside himself with anxiety.

Claire looked down in concern. The woman was conscious, rambling disjointedly, her speech slurred and indistinct. She had little colour in her face at all and her breathing was fast and shallow. As Claire's eyes moved over the tossing figure on the stretcher she realised with horror that the woman was wrapped in a heavy woollen coat, thick lisle stockings and sturdy shoes. She shook her head in disbelief.

'How long have you been in the car?' she asked the man, her fingers already moving to undo the shiny buttons.

'We've come from Melbourne,' he replied, his voice hoarse with worry. 'I suppose we've been on the road for about four hours. We stopped for a cup of tea a couple of hours ago, just before Mother started feeling queer.'

'She's been like this for a couple of hours?'

'More or less. I thought if I could get to Hamilton our daughter would know what to do, but then I got a bit frightened and pulled in here.'

'A good thing too,' Claire agreed. They had wheeled the trolley into an examination cubicle. 'Why on earth is she dressed like this?'

'It's her good coat,' the man said defensively. 'Mother always likes to wear it when we go in the car.'

'And your car's not air-conditioned?'

He shook his head.

While they were talking the two nurses were working

swiftly, stripping the heavy woollen garments from the slight figure on the bed. Peggy turned on the big ceiling fan overhead and Rowena set up another on a bench at the side.

'Is she going to be all right?'

'I think so,' Claire reassured the man. 'I'm glad you stopped here, though. Another hour of that sort of heat could have killed her.' She signalled to Rowena. 'Could you take Mr Robinson and give him a long, cold drink followed by a cup of tea, please, Sister? And remove that sweater from him—forcibly if you have to.' She gave the old man a reassuring smile. 'We'll have her better for you, but it's going to take some time. It'll probably be forty-eight hours before we let her out of here. If you go with Sister MacMillan she'll look after you and help you ring your daughter.'

Rowena led him reluctantly away and left Peggy and Claire to the task of cooling his wife down and getting some fluids into the dangerously dehydrated body.

'How on earth could they travel like that?' Peggy exploded as soon as Mr Robinson was out of earshot.

'They don't feel it,' Claire said seriously, carefully inserting a needle to set up a drip. 'People worry about small children in cars on hot days, but in fact you get a lot more old people in trouble. They have poor circulation and rug up because they're always frightened of being cold.' She motioned to the semi-conscious woman on the trolley. 'This is the result.'

As Claire finished settling the woman she glanced at her watch. Five p. m. She would be finished here soon, but the thought of going back to the farm to spend another night avoiding Alastair dismayed her. She left the examination cubicle to find Rowena beckoning to her from the sister's station.

'It's Rory on the phone. He wants to talk to you.'
She held out the phone, watching Claire appraisingly.
Claire suppressed a grimace of irritation and took the
phone from the outstretched hand.

'Hello, Rory.'

'You're a hard woman to catch.'

'I've been busy.'

'And having a hard time too, I hear.' His tone was
sympathetic. 'Bad luck, Claire. It was a rotten thing to
happen.'

Claire thawed slightly. He might be rich and
indulged, but the sympathy seemed genuine.

'What are you doing tonight?' Rory continued.
'What about coming down to the coast with me?'

'But you can't drive.'

'No, but you do. I've got an air-conditioned little
Alfa which will have us on the Warrnambool beach in
half an hour. You can have a swim while I lie on the
beach and nurse my plaster cast, and then I'll take you
out to dinner. Warrnambool has a couple of good
restaurants, believe it or not.'

Claire hesitated. The plan was definitely appealing.

'I'd have to check and make sure Alastair could be
on call.'

'You do that,' Rory agreed affably. 'Unless I hear
from you I'll expect to see you here in an hour.'

Claire put down the phone and reluctantly went to
find Alastair. He was still in the clinic. She waited until
he had finished with a patient and slipped into his
room.

'You don't need permission from me,' he snapped as
she outlined her plans.

'You were on call yesterday. It hardly seems fair to

leave everything to you again tonight,' she responded stiffly.

'I'm going to have to get used to it. Now,' he walked to the door and held it open, 'if you'll excuse me, I have another patient waiting.'

Despite the burden of guilt weighing her down, Claire enjoyed the trip to the coast. The smart little Alfa was a dream to drive, and Rory set himself out to be his most charming. To her surprise he turned out to be a knowledgeable and informative guide, and Claire relaxed, deliberately soaking in the countryside. If she only had a few more days in the country perhaps she had better make the most of it.

It seemed like only a few minutes before they reached the coast. Rory guided them along a sandy track off the highway before finally directing Claire to park. She climbed out of the car and sniffed appreciatively. The wind was settling with the oncoming dusk. It was still hot, but not oppressive here as it was inland. She could smell the sea, and the waves were pounding enticingly close. Leaving Rory still climbing out of the car, she climbed the low sandhill and gasped in delight. The beach stretched indefinitely before her, a ribbon of golden sand reaching for miles on either side. The waves curled and foamed, breaking to run in cool, frothing fingers up the beach.

Rory was forgotten. Claire had her bathing suit on under her dress. With one swift movement she had rid herself of her dress and was running full tilt into the surf. At knee-depth she dived, emerging gasping and laughing from a foaming breaker.

She looked back up the beach. Rory had appeared over the sand-hill and was settling himself in the dunes to watch her. Claire felt a quick pang of sympathy, then forgot him again as the surf enveloped her. All the tensions and the heat of the last few weeks were put aside as she soaked in the wonderful, wonderful sea.

She emerged an hour later, exhausted but almost happy. Dusk had started to fall and the wind had completely disappeared. She brushed the water from her face and flicked back her streaming hair as she ran up the beach and threw herself down on a towel beside Rory.

'That was fantastic!' She looked up at him and smiled. 'Thank you, Rory. It must have been hell for you to have to sit and watch.'

'I wouldn't describe it as hell.' His eyes moved slowly down the full length of her figure, and Claire flushed. 'I've had worse experiences. Where did you learn to swim like that?'

She sat up and drew a towel around her, suddenly aware of the remoteness of the beach.

'We do have beaches in England too, you know.' She didn't add that swimming had been a compulsory part of her rehabilitation after the crash.

'And surf?'

'And surf,' she said firmly. She towelled herself dry and looked vainly around for cover. 'Be a gentleman and turn your back while I dress,' she demanded.

'I'd rather not.'

'I'll put sand down your plaster cast if you don't,' she retorted. She picked up a handful of sand and aimed it at him. 'Well?'

He looked consideringly at her, then smiled.

'Point to you,' he conceded. 'You have an unfair advantage.'

'Why else do you think I agreed to come with you?' she grinned at him.

They ate at a tiny seafood restaurant overlooking the cliffs near the mouth of the river. Claire entered feeling conscious of her appearance. A light cotton dress and a comb run roughly through her curls were all the preparation she had been able to make. She needn't have worried. Three-quarters of the restaurant's customers appeared to have come straight from the beach.

The food was superb, fish and lobster that tasted as if it had been caught within the last half-hour. Claire found herself struggling to finish her lobster, but refused to leave any on her plate. It would be a long time before she had a luxury like this again.

Waiters hovered discreetly in the background, ensuring their every need was catered for. Rory was well known to the proprietor, and Claire found herself wondering how many other girls he had taken there. Certainly his charm and poise were impeccable. Claire relaxed, enjoying the food and entertained by his witty banter. There was little required on her part as Rory simply demanded an appreciative audience.

She was tired on the drive home. The time in the surf had taken its toll, as well as the last two disturbed and restless nights. She was relieved to finally pull up outside the MacMillans' palatial residence where her old Mercedes was waiting to take her home. She turned to Rory.

'Thank you for a lovely night,' she said sincerely. 'It was just what I needed.'

'The pleasure was mine.' He reached out in the confines of the little car and slipped a hand through her hair. 'Can we do it again soon?'

Claire caught his hand and pulled it away gently. 'I'm sorry, Rory, but we can't. I'm going home on Saturday.'

'Home?' His tone was startled.

'Back to England.'

'But I thought you were here permanently.'

'Only on trial,' she corrected him. 'And the trial didn't work out.'

'Well. . .' he said consideringly. Claire could almost see him doing calculations in his head, reassessing his position. 'Well. If I want you I'm going to have to work fast.'

She shook her head. 'I wouldn't bother. I don't think I'm worth the effort.'

'I think I'm a better judge of that than you are, my lovely.' He reached out swiftly and caught her, dragging her over to him. His face came down on hers and she was caught. As his lips met hers his hands held her unwilling body hard against him, brooking no protest.

For a moment Claire was passive, willing it to be over. A moment, however, was all it took for her to realise it was not going to stop. One hand held her while the other searched, fumbling with the obstruction of her clothes.

She gasped and pulled back, but she was no match for him. She tried to twist to open the car door behind her, but there was no room. The car held her trapped.

'Come on, my lovely,' Rory muttered, his voice thick with passion. 'You want it as much as I do.'

'You've got to be kidding!' Claire wrenched away, but was hauled back across the seats.

'Don't muck me about!' There was excitement and anger in the tone, and she felt a sharp stab of fear. He was a spoiled boy, no more, but with a man's strength when crossed.

Suddenly she felt him stiffen and in relief realised that lights were blazing through the windscreen. She jerked upward. Rowena was standing on the front veranda, a faint smile on her lips. She came slowly down the steps towards them, as Claire struggled to regain some semblance of dignity. Rowena's voice, as she neared the window of the car, was laced with amusement, and Claire wondered just how long she had watched and listened before she had flicked on the lights.

'Alastair's been called back to the hospital. He rang to see if you were back yet. If you can bear to drag yourself away I gather he needs a hand.'

'I. . . Of course.' Claire reached the door-handle and emerged, trying to suppress the awful humiliation she was feeling. She looked briefly back into the darkness of the Alfa. 'Goodnight, Rory.'

There was no reply. Claire shrugged and, without looking at Rowena, made her way over to the Mercedes.

'I'll let Alastair know you're on your way,' Rowena said sweetly.

I'll bet you will! Claire thought savagely. The roar as she revved the engine split the night. With relief she made her way back to the hospital.

Despite her anger she drove slowly to the hospital, trying to regain some composure as she did so. Her cheeks burned with humiliation. How dared Rory maul her as if she were his property? And for Rowena to have found her in such a situation! She pressed a hand up to her forehead. Her temples throbbed and for a moment she thought she was going to have to stop the car to be sick.

With an effort she pulled herself together. Whatever was waiting for her at the hospital could not be dealt with while she was in this frame of mind. She smoothed back her hair from her face and concentrated on the road. At this time of night it was treacherous, with kangaroos often leaping into the path of oncoming cars. Her body was still sticky from the salt water and she ached for a wash. The joy of the swim seemed a long way in the past.

By the time she pulled into the hospital car park Alastair had already parked and was inside. Outside the hospital doors was an ancient fire truck, very dirty and, by the look of it, recently used. Claire frowned, remembering Dorothy's fear of fire. She swung the hospital door open and went in.

Seated on the chairs at the entrance were three characters who were almost comical in their filth. They were blackened with dust and ash, and the smell of fire filled the narrow hall. They looked up at her as she entered, and Claire recognised the signs of exhaustion. Peggy appeared from the sister's station, her face creased with worry.

'It's just minor burns, Claire, but something tells me this is only the beginning.' She threw a white coat towards Claire and disappeared into the examination cubicles. Claire followed.

For the next hour there was little time for worry about the fire itself. The sister on duty had called in Peggy at the same time as she had called Alastair. All of them were fully occupied treating the exhausted men. The men's eyes were the worst affected parts of their bodies, and even after they had been thoroughly washed with saline solution they threatened to be sore for some time to come. The burns were mostly incidental burns caused by flying debris, treated with cool, moist compresses and coated with cream. Only one of the men needed admitting. He was older than the others and was suffering severely from heat exhaustion. Claire treated his minor burns and left Peggy supervising a cool sponge bath.

'Where's the fire?' she heard Alastair ask as he ushered the last man in to be checked.

'It's up the back of Mount Fyans, in the scrub there,' the man replied. 'It started at the railway line. A spark from the rails would be all it took at the moment, I reckon. We tried to stop it before it reached the scrub, but we didn't have a hope.'

Alastair frowned. Claire, finished for the time being, moved to prepare some fresh saline solution. The two nurses were both occupied.

'They're not going to be able to douse it there in a hurry.'

The smoke-stained man shook his head.

'It's there for a while, is my guess. Just as long as the wind doesn't get up in the morning, or we're in real trouble.'

Alastair nodded, his brow creased into a furrow.

'I don't like it.'

'You're telling me,' the other man agreed. He lowered himself from the couch as Alastair finished. 'Thanks, Doc. We'll be getting on.'

'You're not going back there tonight?' asked Claire.

'No.' He grinned at her. 'Reckon the boys have earned a rest for now. There's three other units there. We just got a blast when the wind came up for a moment and swung the fire back on us—gave us all a fright. We'll be more careful tomorrow.'

'Let's hope you don't have to be,' Claire replied. 'Perhaps it'll rain in the night.'

'Perhaps pigs'll fly,' the man retorted. 'See you soon.'

'Not too soon,' Alastair said firmly. 'Go home and give those eyes a rest.'

'Yes, Doc.'

Alastair smiled grimly as she closed the door after him. He and Claire worked in silence as they cleaned up the room.

'I'm sorry I interrupted your evening,' Alastair said eventually, and Claire flushed.

'I wasn't exactly enjoying myself,' she retorted, wondering what Rowena had told him.

He raised his eyebrows in faint disbelief.

'Oh?'

Their eyes met, anger meeting anger. Claire's gaze dropped first. So what if this man didn't believe her? It was nothing to her. He was nothing to her. She looked up again and he was still watching her, the anger giving way to something else. Sadness? Surely not. He held out his hand.

'Claire?'

'No!' She almost screamed the word at him and backed away. The door opened behind her and Peggy re-entered the room.

'There. Everything shipshape again and ready for tomorrow.' She looked curiously from Claire to Alastair, the tension between the two almost a solid presence in the room, but forbore to comment. 'If the worst does come to the worst tomorrow at least they can't accuse us of being unprepared.'

'Let's hope it doesn't come to that,' Claire said stiffly. 'Now, if you'll excuse me I'm going home.'

'You don't want to stay here the night?' Peggy asked.

Claire shook her head. As little as she relished the drive back to the farm, the thought of a bath, cool, clean sheets and, above all, privacy, was enough to overcome her weariness and send her home.

'I'll stay,' Alastair said quietly. 'If there are three units still at the fire it's best if one of us does.'

Claire glanced up at him sharply. 'Are you going to need me? Should I stay?'

He shook his head. 'Go home, Claire. I'll call you back if I have to, but I'd rather Mum wasn't alone.'

She met his gaze. His look was steady, and she felt her heart fill with a deep, raw pain. This man could be everything to her. A sense of hopelessness filled her, an all-enveloping misery. How could she leave this place, leave this man? She dug her hands deep in the pockets of her white coat, gave him one last, long look and turned and fled.

CHAPTER TEN

CLAIRE slept fitfully, but as the sun slowly dawned, she fell finally into a deep slumber. She was roused by Dorothy wheeling in, bearing her breakfast on a tray.

'Oh, Dorothy!' She sat up in bed and rubbed her eyes. 'You shouldn't have bothered.'

'Nonsense.' Dorothy placed the tray carefully on the bedside table and wheeled over to pull the curtains. 'I've suddenly realised how few of these mornings we have left together. Are you still set on leaving us?'

'On Saturday,' Claire affirmed. 'I had Jean book my flight yesterday. I'll catch the train to Melbourne on Friday night.'

Dorothy shook her head. 'I'm going to miss you.'

'Come and visit me, then.' Claire dredged up a smile. 'Get your farm in order, sell some of your prize Herefords for a small fortune and come and visit the old country. I'd enjoy showing you the sights.'

'I'd enjoy seeing them with you.' Dorothy also tried to smile, but it didn't quite come off. 'I just hope I've got the courage to keep going here without you to support me.'

'Of course you have.' Claire put down her teacup and rose, crossing the room to place her hands on the elderly lady's shoulders. 'Alastair will give you all the support you need.'

'Yes. Well, I'm not going to see all that much of Alastair, am I, if he's back to being the only doctor?'

'All the better,' Claire retorted, with a light-heartedness she was far from feeling. 'He won't be able to interfere.' She looked at the bedside clock. 'Good grief!'

'I didn't want to wake you,' Dorothy said apologetically. 'I know what time you came in.'

'Have you heard whether they have the fire under control?'

Dorothy nodded. 'They've still got it contained in the scrub area around Mount Fyans. It'll be OK unless the wind comes up.'

Claire looked out of the window. Hot but still.

'Are you sure you don't want to come in with me today?' she asked, knowing already what the answer would be. 'OK, OK!' she laughed, throwing her hands up in mock defence at the expression on Dorothy's face. 'I was only asking!'

The day stretched interminably. As Claire sat in the clinic she was conscious of an all-pervading sense of weariness. She knew it had little to do with physical tiredness.

She and Alastair treated another couple of fire-fighters for minor problems, but the news they heard from them was reassuring. The area of fire was being slowly diminished as more local farmers joined the effort. If it stayed calm they should have it out by nightfall.

Mid-afternoon Jean entered Claire's room with a worried expression on her face. She handed Claire the next history and made to leave, but Claire stopped her.

'Is something wrong?'

Jean shrugged. 'I'm probably worrying unnecessarily, but I reckon the wind is rising.'

Claire crossed to the window and looked out. The dust in the distant paddocks was stirring and lifting. Was it clouds of dust? All of a sudden she wasn't sure. She turned to Jean and saw her dismay reflected in the other's face.

'That's smoke from Mount Fyans,' Jean almost whispered. 'You can smell it.'

It was there, suddenly, in the room with them, the slight smell of smoke.

'It's probably all right,' Jean said uneasily. 'With the wind like this a little bit of smoke goes a long way. It's just enough to make you a bit edgy.'

'We shouldn't panic yet?'

Jean shook her head and smiled faintly. 'I'll let you know when to panic.'

'Just give me lots of notice so I can get myself properly worked up,' Claire demanded. 'Meanwhile I guess we'd better keep going.'

Jean crossed to the door to call the next patient, Mrs Burrows, only to find her already standing.

'If you don't mind, Doctor,' she said apologetically to Claire, 'I'm going to get on home. I don't like this. I'm going to turn on the pumps and fill the spouts.' She left, her complaints put aside until more urgent matters were dealt with.

The smell of smoke evoked reaction from nearly all the patients seated in the waiting-room. With a couple of urgent exceptions the patients departed, and those who were left wanted to be treated in a hurry, so they also were free to take precautions. There was no time for pleasant banter. Soon Alastair, Jean and Claire were left standing in a deserted waiting-room.

'Would you like to go home to the farm?' Claire asked Alastair.

He shook his head. 'No. The wind is coming in this direction from Mount Fyans. If the fire breaks loose it'll be the town that's threatened. Our farm will be out of its path. I'm going to spend this lull spreading a bit of water around here.'

'Wouldn't the garden protect the hospital?' Claire asked, her gaze surveying the pleasant greenery in view from the clinic door.

'To a certain extent, yes,' Alastair agreed. 'All it needs is a few sparks on the roof and in the gutters, though. I'll block the gutters and fill them with water.' He left them.

Claire and Jean were left looking at each other in dismay.

'Come on,' Jean said decisively. 'We're going to feel stupid doing this if nothing happens, but I think the situation warrants it.'

'What are we going to do?'

'We're going to get some necessary equipment down to the river. When the fire came through fifteen years ago the only safe place was sitting in the swimming hole with a wet blanket over your head. If we have to evacuate the hospital that's where we'll take them. Let's get some gear down there just in case. At worst, or I guess I should say at best, we'll just have to lug it back again.'

They took three trips down to the river bank. A couple of the elderly nursing home residents shook off their debility and volunteered to help. Claire and Jean loaded up the hospital van with blankets and medical necessities and unloaded them beside the water. Flushed with importance, the two elderly men fussed around, organising the equipment so it stayed clean and dry until needed. As the smell of the smoke grew

stronger and the sound of an approaching siren signalled the end of their period of quiet, Claire and Jean
returned to the hospital, satisfied that should the need
arise everything was ready.

'And if it doesn't, Mr Jarvis and Mr Henty are going
to be two disappointed men,' Jean said, and Claire
laughed.

It was the last time she laughed for quite a while. The
siren signalled the approach of an ambulance, bearing
exhausted, smoke-covered fire-fighters. As Claire
moved from one to the next she was amazed to find
women among the battle-weary group.

'It's our homes too,' one of the girls said as Claire
washed out her eyes. 'You don't think we'd just sit and
cheer while our men do the hard work?'

Claire shook her head in admiration. There wasn't
an idle hand in the district. If ever a community
deserved to survive this one did.

'Oh, we'll survive all right,' Peggy said as she
replaced Claire's saline solution. 'It's just a matter of
how many buildings we've got left standing. The community doesn't depend on buildings.'

Brave words, thought Claire as she washed and
rewashed the girl's painful eyes. As she looked around
the casualty ward and saw the deep worry etched into
the faces around her she couldn't help wondering how
many livelihoods depended on the fire-fighters' efforts.

'What about your farm?' she asked Peggy.

'I've got a husband and five sons,' Peggy retorted. 'If
they can't manage to save the house and the stock
without me there's something wrong with them.'
Almost under her breath she muttered, 'They'd better.'

Inside the hospital they were protected from the

gradual darkening of the sky as the smoke and dust billowed and swirled, blocking the light. As the squeal of tyres signalled the approach of more patients Claire and Alastair went outside, and Claire drew in her breath at the unaccustomed gloom.

'The fire's still a fair way off,' Alastair said reassuringly. 'This wind is sending the smoke a long way fast.'

'Are you sure Dorothy will be safe?' Claire demanded. The thought of her friend watching this alone from her front veranda unsettled her.

He gave a grimace. 'I'd rather she were here, I'll admit, but she won't come. I phoned her half an hour ago and said I'd send someone to get her, but she won't have it. If the wind stays heading this way she'll be safe. The town's in a direct line, but the farm's not.'

'Will it get this far?'

'They're trying to stop it at the railway line,' Alastair replied. 'The highway's the next break after that. If it crosses the highway, we evacuate.'

He stopped abruptly as they reached the car that had just pulled up. A white-faced woman nursing a little girl was in the back. Held tightly in the child's arms was a puppy.

'They've lost their farm,' the driver explained briefly. 'It was right in the path of the fire. They got to the dam all right, but the little one remembered the pup and took off after it. Found it too,' he said admiringly, 'but she's got some burns to her legs and arms.'

He helped the shocked woman out and Alastair gently took the child from her. A quick inspection showed the burns to be mainly superficial. Shcok was the main worry.

Jean moved in with a blanket to wrap around the shivering woman. Although not a nurse she was doing a nurse's job as they all worked to capacity. Alastair took the little girl into an examination cubicle and Jean followed with her mother. There was no attempt to remove the puppy. For now the little group needed each other.

There was another man in the passenger seat of the car, an elderly man suffering from smoke inhalation. Claire supervised as the stretcher was brought into the hospital. She checked his throat for respiratory tract burns, organised oxygen for him and then found herself temporarily idle. Peggy emerged from the examination cubicle, where Alastair was still treating the little girl.

'Is she all right?' asked Claire. 'Does Alastair need help?'

Peggy shook her head. 'They'll be fine. Alastair's given the mum a sedative. I'll pop them up in a ward together when he's finished.'

'With the puppy?'

'With the puppy,' Peggy said decisively. 'I'm the matron here and I can break any rules I want.' She walked to the door and looked out. The sky was black and filled with debris. 'I wish I knew what was happening.'

Rowena appeared from the wards behind them. 'Peggy, I'm going home.'

Peggy whirled around. 'You're needed here, Rowena.'

Rowena looked pointedly at her watch. 'It's four o'clock and officially I'm off duty. I don't like Dad's chances of keeping the ponies calm in this,' she gestured to the sky, 'and Rory can't help with his broken ankle. If they panic they could injure themselves.'

'And what if I have to evacuate the hospital?' Peggy said icily.

'You've got enough people here to do that without me,' Rowena replied calmly.

'Rowena!' Alastair called out to her as he emerged from the examination cubicle. Rowena stood waiting, her eyebrows raised in faint enquiry. 'Are you going back to your place?'

Rowena nodded. Alastair came forward and gripped her arm.

'Could you stop at Ardlethan and take Mum with you? I don't like her being out there by herself.'

'Sure,' she said easily, and flashed a triumphant smile at Peggy. 'Glad to be of service.' She ran lightly down to the car park.

The lull came to an end almost immediately as another car-load of fire-fighters arrived. Claire was brought forcibly in mind of a war zone. Bring them in, patch them up and send them out to fight again, she thought grimly, then chastised herself at the comparison. So far the injuries were only trivial.

Half an hour later the news was good. The wind seemed to be dropping and the fire was being held at the highway. Jean's and Claire's preparations at the river bank looked like being unnecessary, for which Claire was profoundly grateful. The thought of immersing a hospital full of patients in the swimming hole was horrific. With the news a feeling of relief seemed to sweep through the staff. The workload didn't get any lighter, though. Casualty patients arrived in a steady stream.

Alastair and Claire worked efficiently, the burden of worry lessened with the news that the threat of evacuation had eased. Still, though, the gloom of smoke hung over the hospital, making it impossible to relax completely. Every time the main door opened their eyes would lift. New casualties meant more work and news of the fire.

A fast car swept into the car park. Tuned to listening for vehicles, Claire and Alastair exchanged glances. A vehicle travelling at speed probably spelled trouble. Alastair turned from the patient he was treating and, as he did so, the hospital door burst open. A tall, stooped man in his early forties entered, his white shirt and tie differentiating him from the fire-fighters they were used to seeing.

'Sam Cray!' Alastair's voice was both welcoming and relieved. 'What on earth are you doing here?' He came forward and gripped the stranger's hand. 'Claire, this is Dr Cray, who acted as a locum here while I went to England.'

Claire paused and looked up from the hands she was bandaging. She smiled at the pleasant, open-faced man she saw before her.

'So you're Alastair's next victim.' Sam grinned. 'He talked me into working for him too. Never again——'

'What are you doing here?' Alastair demanded, cutting him short.

Sam held his hands out expressively. 'To work, dear boy. Having said never again, here I am.' His glance took in the scene and his expression became serious. 'In fact, I've been listening to the radio for most of the day. By lunchtime it was clear you were in trouble, so I ditched my comfortable city patients with all their associated neuroses for the afternoon, and here I am. They'll still be waiting when I get back. They might have even dredged up some new symptoms,' he added.

Alastair nodded, his eyes reflecting his pleasure at his friend's arrival.

'What do you say, Claire? Can we use him?'

Claire taped off the bandage she was winding and rose to her feet. 'We certainly can.' She smiled, and gestured to the bench where five people were waiting to be seen. 'Where would you like to start?'

Sam's arrival meant that for the first time in the afternoon the workload started to come under control. By the time the ambulance's siren was heard again the queue waiting for attention had disappeared. Just as well, thought Claire as they checked the two new arrivals. One of the men came in clutching his arm in agony, and a swift examination revealed a hand that was limp and bloodless. A compound fracture of the man's elbow had blocked the artery. If he wasn't going to lose his arm they were going to have to perform emergency surgery.

Claire opted out. Sam was happy to give the anaesthetic and Claire was relieved to hand the responsibility over to him. It was getting late and she was more tired than she cared to admit. Alastair and Sam disappeared into the theatre, and Claire turned to treat the minor burns of the man's companion.

'How did this happen?' she asked him. 'I thought the fire was almost under control.'

'Not any more it's not,' the man said grimly. 'We were on the edge of the fire. It was being held at the highway and we were working in from the edges.' He gestured outside. 'That was OK until the wind swung around. It came straight back at us. We had the truck with us and tried to outrun it. We hit a stump, which is how Charlie broke his arm. There was another truck coming up behind us or we'd have been goners.'

Claire looked down at him with horror. 'You mean it's no longer being held?'

He shook his head. 'It's out of control now, that's for sure. Not heading for the town, though.'

She stood silently for a momnt, then looked outside at the rustling branches. The wind was north-east. If the fire was moving from the highway. . .

'Ardlethan will be in its path.'

The man looked up at her. 'I reckon you're right. The MacMillans' too.'

Claire swung round in horror to find Peggy listening in concern to the conversation.

'Dorothy's alone out there.'

Peggy nodded, her eyes mirroring Claire's horror.

'Rowena was going over,' Claire remembered. 'She'll have her at the MacMillans'.' She stopped and looked almost pleadingly at Peggy, wanting the matron to reassure her.

'Would you trust Rowena to spend time fetching Dorothy when her precious polo ponies are in danger?' Peggy said slowly. 'I think we should get Alastair.'

Claire shook her head. She looked around. There was no one waiting to be seen. For the moment she was free.

'No—that elbow is a tricky piece of surgery. I don't think I'm competent to take over.' She walked over to the desk and grabbed her car keys. 'Get on to the fire units if you can. See if one of them can be diverted. I'm going.' She ran out before Peggy or the fire-fighter she had been treating could find words to argue.

The drive to the farm was a nightmare. Claire drove as fast as she dared, but the dense smoke had visibility down to nearly zero. She had to slow to almost a crawl and could have screamed with frustration. There was no way of telling where the fire itself was. There were no flames visible from the road, but that in itself wasn't reassuring. It would have to be ten feet away before you could see it, Claire thought. Finally she stopped at Ardlethan's road gate. She climbed out and left it open as she restarted the engine and gunned the old car down the drive. If stock got out on to the road perhaps they had a chance rather than being trapped in a paddock.

She pulled up in front of the house with a screech of brakes and put her hand firmly on the horn. Nothing. Suddenly from round the back of the house raced Rusty and Red, and Claire's heart sank. Surely if Rowena had persuaded Dorothy to leave she wouldn't have left the dogs behind? She gave the dogs a quick reassuring pat and they followed her nervously as she entered the house.

There was no Dorothy. Claire ran from room to room, calling, the dogs not leaving her side. She picked up the phone. Dead.

For a moment she succumbed to panic, blind, irrational panic. Outside the smoke was building up, slowly permeating the house. As she stood in the hall she could see it, swirling and creeping in through the door. How close was the fire? Perhaps Dorothy really was at the MacMillans'. She closed her eyes, trying to control her rising hysteria. One of the dogs pushed his cool, moist nose into the palm of her hand, and the contact with another living thing steadied her. She looked down at the nervous dog and her mind started working again.

They had been outside, around the back of the house, when she arrived. Why? If Dorothy was here and it was at all possible they would have been with her. Cursing herself for her stupidity, she ran out through the kitchen, the dogs following.

They left her as soon as she was out of the screen door, racing ahead towards the machinery shed. Claire followed them through the smoke, yelling at the same time.

'Dorothy!'

At last she heard what she had been praying for.

'Over here—in the shed!'

Dorothy was lying on the floor of the shed, and one swift glance told Claire what had happened. Beside her was the petrol-driven generator. Dorothy had been trying to get it started, leaned too far forward and toppled out of her chair.

'Oh, my dear, am I pleased to see you!' Dorothy's voice was husky from fright. 'I thought——' Her voice broke off.

'I thought too,' Claire said grimly. Dorothy lifted her arms and Claire reached down to pull her back into the chair. 'Come on, let's get to the dam.'

'No.' Dorothy had regained her poise and was back in control. 'We've got a little time. The smoke will get denser than this before the fire's here. Besides, I can't hear anything.'

'Hear anything?' Claire queried.

'We'll hear the flames before we can see them,' Dorothy said firmly. 'Claire, can you get this machine going? All you have to do is pull the starter motor— the same as a lawn-mower.'

'Why?' Claire was reaching for the starter as she spoke.

'The water pump is electrically driven.' The roar of the motor starting cut across Dorothy's words and she had to yell the remainder. 'The electricity has been cut. No generator, no water.'

With the generator running Claire pulled the wheelchair out of the shed and back towards the house.

Dorothy signalled towards a hose lying at the back door, now gushing water.

'I was respraying the roof when the power went off. Give me the hose and I'll keep going. Claire?'

'Yes?'

'There are two things left to do, if we've time. There's a flock of sheep in the top paddock, crowded against the fence. If the fire comes through they'll be burnt. If you can open the gate they'll get down the drive and on to the road. At least that way they've got a chance.'

Claire shook her head. 'How do I get them to come through the gate?'

'Use the dogs. Just tell them to get away back and they should get behind them and drive them through. It depends how much authority you can put into your voice.' While Dorothy was talking she was sending a shower of water arcing over the tin roof.

'And the other thing?'

'On the dining table there's a pile of things I sorted this morning.' Suddenly Dorothy's voice trembled and Claire bent to hear. 'I'd hate to lose them. We've got a hole dug in the kitchen garden. If there's time could you put as many in the hole as you can? If you shove some earth back over it they should be safe.' She ended on a note of almost pleading. Claire didn't reply. She was already running.

She called the dogs as she went and they came with her, two silent shadows. As she came out of the lee of the back of the house she gasped. The smoke was pea-soup thick. She put out a hand to try and ward off the stinging stuff reaching her eyes. As she ran she tripped and tripped again. It was hard to see the ground.

Finally she put a hand through each of the dogs' collars. It kept her steady and gave her a sense of security.

The sheep were there, bunched hard up against the gate, immobile in their terror. Claire reached through and released the chain, then swung the gate wide. The flock wavered and moved back, away from the gate.

Claire released the dogs and spoke as firmly as she could.

'Get away back!'

The dogs stirred uneasily and looked at her. She obviously didn't have the right tone. Taking a deep breath, she steadied herself and tried again.

'Get away back!'

The dogs went, darting towards the rear of the flock. Claire moved back, away from the open gate, and the sheep surged through. Once through there was nothing between them and the drive, and past the drive the roadway beyond. They disappeared quickly from view, and Claire sent a silent blessing after them. There was nothing else she could do for them. She called the dogs back to her sides and ran back to the house.

The things Dorothy had spoken of were piled high in readiness, with plastic bags beside them. Claire threw the items into the bags. There was no time to worry about breakables, but in the main they seemed fairly robust—photo albums, trophies, picture frames, prize ribbons. She heaved the bags outside. Dorothy was still there, spraying water with grim determination. She directed Claire to the hole, and Claire threw the bags into the pit. There was a shovel beside it and a mound of fresh earth, obviously prepared for just such an eventuality. In seconds a layer of earth covered the precious belongings.

Dorothy was starting to cough with the smoke as

Claire returned to her, but she pulled herself together to rasp out, 'There's still time—I can't hear it yet. Get some sensible shoes on.'

Claire glanced down at her footwear and started to run inside again. Thin sandals were going to be useless. She pulled open her wardrobe and grabbed a woollen shirt, a pair of trousers and leather boots. It was the fastest change she had ever made in her life.

Thinking of Jean and the preparations she had made at the river, Claire seized a couple of thick woollen blankets from the chest beside the bed. She did a lightning check to ensure that the windows and doors were shut. As she checked the lounge-room window she looked out at the gloom. For a second she thought the smoke was clearer, and then she saw a thin orange line. She ran.

Dorothy had propped the hose, still spraying on to the roof, carefully laying it on concrete all the way from the tap, and had turned her chair to go. She had heard what Claire had seen. Claire shoved the blankets on to her lap and got behind the chair. She pushed while Dorothy turned the wheels with her hands.

The dam was only a short distance from the house, but Claire would remember that run for as long as she lived. Heat was blasting at them from behind like a roaring furnace, driving them on. Claire slowed slightly, checking their frantic haste. A fall now would be fatal.

Finally the dam wall loomed out of the blackness. She turned the chair and pulled it backwards, up and over the bank. It reached the peak and then ran itself, Claire guiding its path, down into the water.

Dorothy slid out of the chair herself into the cool murkiness of the water, catching at one of the dogs for support. She was coughing, gasping for breath. Claire was struggling for breath herself. She shoved the chair a little away from them, soaked the blankets and pulled them over their heads. The two dogs, whining in fear, nosed their way under the dripping canopy. Claire and Dorothy each held one, burying their faces into the dogs' damp fur. There was nothing to do now except wait.

Claire had no idea how long they stayed there. She blotted the fire from her consciousness and concentrated on the only two things that mattered, keeping the blankets wet and getting enough air from the smoke-filled tent of the blankets. She heard herself making little crooning noises of reassurance to the dog, and grimaced. Who was more frightened, she or the dog? She held out a hand in the water towards Dorothy and felt it grasped and held. One breath after another.

Gradually the heat receded. The roar of the flames settled and faded. Tentatively the blankets were lifted and Dorothy and Claire emerged.

To Claire, shocked and stunned, their survival in the black-rimmed crater of the dam was the only important thing, but Dorothy was made of sterner stuff.

'Go on, Claire. I'm fine now. See if you can save the house.'

Claire looked at her blankly.

'Go on.' Dorothy gave her a push. 'If the house is still standing you just need to put out the spot fires around it. It must be—you'd still hear the sound of flames if it had gone up.'

She spoke firmly, but Claire heard the note of desperation in her voice, a trembling which showed just how important her home was to her.

'OK, I'll go. Don't you move.'

'Where do you think I'd go?' Dorothy asked mirth-lessly. 'Rusty and Red and I will stay here.' She looked consideringly around at the teeming water. 'As well as every rabbit, snake and bird on the place, by the look of it.'

It was true. The dam was alive with wildlife, none of it posing a threat to the others. For now all that mattered to each was the refuge that the water provided. Claire didn't stop to appreciate the scene, however. She pulled herself out of the water and climbed the still smouldering bank.

'It's still there!' she yelled. Through the haze the house was still standing, surrounded by a vast expanse of blackened earth. Claire cast one last look down at Dorothy, and sensed rather than saw the tremulous joy light her face.

Heat was starting to seep through the soles of her thick boots. She moved quickly off the smouldering earth and on to the relative cool of the track. She was back at the house in minutes. The hose that Dorothy had left was still sending up its spray. Claire used it to go around the house, putting out the small patches of flame licking intermittently in the grass and shrubs against the house. Periodically she raised it to send more jets of water streaming to the roof. Burning debris was still being carried in the wind.

She had been working for fifteen minutes before she heard help arriving. A car was being driven down the track, far faster than was safe. She looked up as Alastair's car skidded to a halt in the driveway.

The smoke was still shrouding the scene. Claire could make out the car with its headlights boring through the haze, but he could not see her. He left the car and started running towards the house.

'Claire! Mum!' His voice was hoarse with fear.

Claire opened her mouth to respond, but no words came out. The adrenalin which had been keeping her going for the past couple of hours suddenly ceased its flow. Her legs turned to jelly beneath her and it was all she could do not to sink on to the charred ground in a faint. She held grimly on to the hose, directing the jet of water high on to the roof. It was all she could think of to do.

As Alastair reached the door he stopped. The water was drumming on the iron roof. He came slowly back down the steps and through the swirling smoke until he reached her.

'Claire?' He reached out a hand to touch her, but Claire didn't respond. The most important thing in the world was to direct the water high above them. She concentrated on the water jet. Nothing else mattered.

'Claire!' He gripped her arm and she turned to look at him, then back to the water. He swore, then pulled the hose forcibly from her grasp and threw it aside. The force of the water left it snaking violently across the smouldering grass, but he ignored it.

'Where's Mum?' He was shaking her now.

From a long way away Claire heard herself answer. Her voice was someone else's.

'She's in the dam. She's all right.' She reached down and seized the writhing hose and centred the stream on to a smouldering shrub beside the house.

Alastair stood watching her for a long moment, but for Claire he had ceased to exist. She only had room for one thing in her mind, and that had to be the water. When he went she was only dimly aware that he had left her, turning to run across the rough track to the dam wall.

When he returned Dorothy was with him. He pushed the chair up the ramp beside the veranda steps and inside. Finally he emerged and came across to the slight smoke-stained figure standing alone in the ruins of the front garden.

Claire was no longer functioning in anything but a mechanical mode. The water still sprayed, but she couldn't direct the jets with any accuracy because of the savage tremors sweeping over her body. Tears were running down her face, leaving paths where they cut through the accumulated grime.

Alastair gently took the hose away from her. He surveyed the front of the house. Claire's dousing had been thorough. For the time being the house seemed secure. He turned back to the trembling figure and picked her up in his arms, cradling her as one would a hurt child. For a long moment he stood, looking down at the unresponsive figure he held. She lay limply in his arms, aware only that the awful responsibility was ended. From the veranda Rusty and Red whimpered in distress and confusion. Alastair looked up from the burden in his arms, his face a mixture of conflicting emotions. His eyes dropped again, and if Claire had been conscious of his gaze it would have told her all she needed to know. She was lost, though, in a misty world of exhaustion and relief. All she knew was that she was being held in arms that held her safe against the world. She nestled softly against him. With an effort Alastair tore his gaze from her face and strode purposefully into the house.

CHAPTER ELEVEN

CLAIRE woke to the smell of smoke. For a moment the nightmare closed in on her again, and as she struggled to sit up panic washed over her. Then her eyes took in her bedroom, clean, neat and normal. She lay back under the crisp sheets, trying to remember.

The events of the night before were hazy. She vaguely remembered Alastair bringing her inside, and then the house seemed to fill with people. It passed into a blur. How had she got into bed? She did a quick inspection of her body. She was clean. Perhaps she'd had a bath. She didn't remember.

She pulled back the covers and tried to rise. Pain radiated upward, a grinding ache from her weak hip and a sharper burning from her calves. She sat down again on the bed and surveyed her legs with detached interest. They were burnt and blistered. She grimaced and looked around for her clothes. In the corner was a pile of disreputable rags—a blackened shirt; boots with the rubber soles melted into misshapen, grotesque forms; jeans, charred and tattered.

Trying again, she pulled herself up and moved stiffly and painfully to the window. She pulled back the curtains and drew her breath in horror.

For as far as she could see the country was black. The charred earth was barren. Burnt trees stood stark against the horizon and in the foreground fence posts still smouldered. For as far as she could see there was no living thing.

Claire forgot the pain in her legs. As if in a dream she left the bedroom and walked out to the veranda. Dorothy was there, staring numbly out across the paddocks.

As she reached her, Claire looked across towards the driveway where she had parked the car last night. The old Mercedes was there, a burnt-out shell.

'Oh, Dorothy.'

The older woman glanced up at her and then in the direction she was looking. She reached up and took Claire's hand.

'I know—I saw it last night. It doesn't matter.'

'But you loved it.'

'It was a friend.' Dorothy admitted. 'And it brought you home to me when I needed you most. What more can I ask of a friend than that?' Claire looked wonderingly down and saw tears sliding down Dorothy's cheeks. She crouched down and hugged her hard. For a moment Dorothy stiffened, then suddenly her arms were around Claire and she wept.

Claire held her until the worst of the racking sobs eased, then she sank to sit beside the wheelchair on the bare wooden veranda boards. They sat there for a long time, both in their nightwear, trying to come to terms with what had happened.

'Is Alastair at the hospital?' Claire asked finally.

Dorothy nodded. 'He had to go back last night and hasn't been home since. He organised one of the fire units to keep a watch here. Someone's been here all night making sure this place didn't go up while we slept.'

'We're safe now, surely?'

'I think everything burning near the house is out.' Dorothy dredged up the ghost of a grin. 'And we've got the best fire-break I've ever seen protecting us now.' She gestured out to the charred horizon.

'Has there been much damage in the district?' asked Claire.

'Fifteen homes gone. No lives lost, praise be, but massive stock loss.' Dorothy closed her eyes and shook her head.

Claire nodded soundlessly.

'One piece of good news,' Dorothy looked up determinedly. 'The flock of sheep you let out were found three kilometres away, grazing safely on the edge of the road. The farmer who found them is keeping them until the MacMillans can collect them.'

Claire smiled, suddenly immeasurably cheered by the news.

'And the fire?'

'Under control. Another wind change in the night drove it back on itself, which was the best thing that could have happened.'

Claire stirred. 'I guess I'd better be getting in to the hospital. They'll be needing me.'

'They don't want you,' Dorothy said firmly. 'Alastair said you were not to move from here with your legs in that state. He's left cream and bandages for you.'

'How did he know my legs were burnt?'

'Who do you think put you to bed?' Dorothy asked, with a trace of her wicked grin.

Claire gazed at her blankly and then flushed. 'I don't know—I can't remember.'

Dorothy smiled. 'We were as helpless as each other last night. When I said it wasn't proper for him to be helping you he threatened to take you to hospital. I thought you'd consider it the lesser of two evils.'

Claire nodded helplessly. She turned away and looked at the blackened landscape. 'Will it ever recover?'

'You wait and see,' Dorothy said firmly. 'Come the autumn rains and the black will disappear like magic.'

'But the trees. . .'

'They regenerate,' Dorothy said firmly, 'at least, most of them do. Australian trees seem to be able to withstand a fire or two.'

Claire shook her head.

'It's true,' Dorothy affirmed. 'Just watch.'

'I can't,' Claire said softly. 'I'm going home.'

Dorothy looked sharply over at her, but bit her lip and said nothing. Claire rose stiffly and went inside. Why should she feel so miserable about missing the first shoots of green in the fire-blackened paddocks?

Peggy dropped in late in the afternoon. Claire was lying on her bed, trying to concentrate on a book, but was finding it impossible. After the hectic pace of the last few days the forced inactivity made her feel guilty. She was delighted to greet Peggy. Dorothy was asleep. She was wearing a brave face, but the shock of the day before's ordeal was still showing.

'I've been told I have to inspect your legs,' Peggy said firmly. 'Let's have 'em.'

Claire protested laughingly. 'You've got more important things to do than worry about my legs! I've only got minor burns. Thank heavens Dorothy told me to take my sandals off, otherwise it might have been a different story. Tell me, though, is your farm safe?'

'The fire didn't reach us,' Peggy said seriously. 'We were one of the lucky ones.'

'And the MacMillans'? I can see from here that they've suffered some damage.'

Peggy sniffed. 'Well, they've lost pasture and some stock. None of their precious ponies, though, I hear. Rowena didn't report for work today—I think she's scared of meeting Alastair.'

Claire shook her head. 'She didn't even try to contact Dorothy. Dorothy kept expecting someone to come, and no one did.'

They sat silently for a while, each unable to voice what they were thinking. If Peggy hadn't doubted Rowena. . . If Claire hadn't come. . . It didn't bear thinking of.

'I wonder where this leaves Rowena and Alastair?' Peggy mused.

'I wonder,' Claire echoed dully. The relationship between Rowena and Alastair failed to interest her any more. They could do what they liked.

Alastair came home late that evening and brought Sam Cray with him. The rush at the hospital had subsided. Claire sat passively at the dinner table, content to sit and listen to the conversation of those around her. She roused slightly when she realised Sam had agreed to return as Alastair's new partner.

'I know I'm going to be overworked.' He grinned. 'I couldn't believe the pace when Alastair was away. My wife's going to be horrified, but I guess she's been expecting it. After working here I haven't been able to settle into a city practice, and when I heard of the fire I suddenly realised where my heart was. You're going to be able to go home with a clear conscience, Claire.'

Claire smiled mechanically, wondering why the news gave her no joy at all. There was now no reason for Alastair to persuade her to stay.

'Sam's offered to stay on until the weekend,' Alastair volunteered. He looked at Claire, who was fiddling uninterestedly with the food on her plate. 'He's got to go back to Melbourne after that to sort out his affairs, but in the meantime I thought I'd take the next couple of days off. The hospital will be quiet. Anybody who's not desperately sick will be far too busy to spend time at the surgery. I'll spend tomorrow getting the urgent repairs done to the fences around the house, and on Friday I'll take you to Port Campbell and then along the Great Ocean Road to catch the plane at Melbourne on Saturday. It seems a pity to go home without seeing our most spectacular scenery.'

'There's no need to put yourself out for me,' Claire said dully. 'I can catch the train.'

She was stopped by Dorothy. From the other side of the table she reached across and gripped Claire's hand in hers.

'There is a need,' she said urgently. 'Allow Alastair to do this much for you. We owe you so much we can never repay it.'

Claire looked across at the three faces watching her with concern, and suddenly she couldn't bear it. This was how it would end—a token gesture from Alastair made out of gratitude. She fought for composure and lost. She pushed her plate back and rose, knocking her chair over in the process. Sam rose and picked it up for her, watching her gravely, and she made a gesture of thanks.

'I. . . I'm sorry, I guess I'm just tired. If you'll excuse me. . .' She backed away blindly from the table, then turned and fled.

The next day dragged. The whole community was frantically busy, and Claire felt like an intruder, packing and preparing to walk away from this disaster area. She packed her suitcases, cleaned up her room and then tried to assist in the house-cleaning necessary to shift the fine layer of ash lying over everything. Her legs were too painful to allow her to do much. Dorothy was more mobile in her wheelchair. They worked together in strained silence, each concerned about saying the wrong thing. Finally a load of fence posts arrived, and Dorothy wheeled thankfully outside.

'I'm not having them put the gate back where it was,' she explained. 'If I've got to have a new fence I might as well take the opportunity to get things right. Besides,' she threw the damp duster she was holding aside, 'I hate housework.'

Claire smiled, but Dorothy was already gone. Claire wandered outside, but felt in the way. Finally she took a spade and went around to the kitchen garden to dig up the treasures she had buried there two days before. She carted the big plastic bags into the kitchen and unpacked them.

She took the photo albums out first and checked them for damp before placing them back in the lounge-room bookshelves. Then there were all the official papers from the farm, followed by the trophies, the prizes and ribbons collected over the generations the Drummond family had run the Hereford stud. It's all ended, Claire thought sadly. Even if Dorothy did get her Herefords back again it would only be for a short while, until age made the running of the farm impossible. Then Rowena would have her way and the farm would be absorbed into the MacMillans'. There would be no more prize Drummond Herefords.

If I stayed it could continue, Claire thought wistfully. With Alastair and me supporting her we could get it going again, make it what it was. And perhaps in time our children. . . Here she stopped. There was no joy in this kind of thinking.

Finally there were the framed photos. Claire took them out and polished them. She found herself looking at a photo of a much younger Dorothy, seated beside her husband with a tiny Alastair on her lap. Claire looked down at the child. His eyes were already laughing, creased in enjoyment of life. Alastair's child could look like that. Tears were slipping stupidly down her cheeks, and she brushed them away impatiently. The sooner she got on a plane for England, the sooner she could leave this stupid version of Claire Bannon behind.

She glanced out of the window. Dressed in jeans, a torn shirt and a bushman's hat, Alastair was pounding the stumps of the remaining fence posts loose with a sledgehammer. For a moment Claire allowed herself the bitter comfort of watching him. The old resolution she had made when she was seventeen came back. It was made in just such a moment of pain. All she could do now was reaffirm that vow. Maybe she could go to one of the countries crying out for medical assistance, Ethiopia or perhaps Bangladesh. Immersed in her work and genuinely needed, maybe in time she could lose this dreadful ache within her.

Claire's leavetaking the next morning was stiff and formal. If she said any of the things she wanted to say to Dorothy she would have broken down.

'I'll write,' she whispered as she climbed into the car beside Alastair. She looked straight ahead, hoping Dorothy would understand.

Dorothy pushed the chair back to rest beside Sam Cray, who would be staying at the farm during the night that Alastair would be away. Sam and his family had stayed with Dorothy while Alastair was in England, so they were old friends. She also seemed to be unable to find the words to say goodbye. As Alastair brought the car to life, Dorothy gripped Sam's hand and the two stood watching as the car disappeared down the long driveway.

There was no gate to open. Like the rest of the fences the road gate had disappeared in Tuesday's inferno. As they turned into the road, Claire turned her head back and raised her hand in a forlorn gesture of farewell to the two receding figures, still hand in hand beside the house.

There was silence in the car. If Claire had to say anything she was going to weep, and she was determined she was not going to let Alastair know how moved she was. It was her decision to leave, and she was doing it for all the right reasons. Alastair could never know what it was costing her.

She hadn't left the farm since the fire, and the state of the countryside was enough to take her mind off her own sadness. The devastation was horrific. They drove through kilometre after kilometre of scorched countryside. Fences no longer existed. Wire hung at crazy angles, supported now and then by the charred stump of a fence post. The massive gums were blackened skeletons with little to show for their former glory except their intact huge trunks. Claire thought back to what Dorothy had said about regeneration and sent up a silent prayer that she might be right.

On the main intersections massive pits had been dug and men and machines waited for loads of carcasses to be brought for burial. Claire and Alastair passed a tray truck with its grim load destined for one of the pits, and Claire turned quickly away, sick with horror. Alastair glanced down at her compassionately but said nothing.

The road was more crowded than she could ever remember. The area was alive with activity. As they passed each burnt property there were scores of people, clearing, fencing, and, in a couple of instances, already building.

'You don't know the value of a community until something like this happens,' Alastair said gently. 'Within hours of the fire, every burnt-out family had a caravan or alternative accommodation to use, and now there are teams of builders making sure everyone's got a reasonable roof over their heads. The proper rebuilding can't start until the insurance assessors go through, but,' he indicated a couple of groups of men clustered around a burnt shell of a farmhouse, men whose clothing signified them as city rather than farm folk, 'most of the insurance will be assessed by the end of the week. New homes will be going up within a month.'

'They've lost so much,' whispered Claire.

Alastair nodded. 'It's the little things that hurt most—the photos, the old battered teddy. But people are amazingly generous. We had five new bicycles dropped in to the hospital last night for us to give to children who'd lost theirs. In a community like this there's always a sense of, next time it could be me, or last time it was me. As far as the community can we'll make sure people don't suffer.'

Claire was silent. The enormity of the last two days' events overwhelmed her.

They dropped into the hospital to allow her to say goodbye. She gave Peggy a brief, hard hug and left quickly. Surely she had been here for longer than a month. It seemed. . . The words sprang unbidden to her mind. It seems like home.

Away from the hospital the countryside changed. A long line marked the end of the fire's path and the country reverted to its normal brown. Claire blinked unbelievingly. Here, life was normal. What decreed where the line should be? For the rest of the drive she sat and marvelled at each unburnt house, each area of unburnt bush. The land became undulating as they neared the coast. On small, picturesque farms dairy herds were peacefully grazing, and Claire had to suppress an urge to pinch herself to see if she was dreaming, so great was the contrast.

A sweeping curve and Port Campbell was before them. It was a tiny town, nestled in the cove created by two massive cliff faces breaking their line to curve and form the natural mouth to a wide, shallow river. The river was tiny now in comparison to those towering cliffs. Beside the mouth of the river was a stretch of golden sand, and, further out as the cliffs started, was a jetty, its access road blasted from the rock by men determined to find a place to launch their fishing boats. The place was breathtakingly beautiful.

It was deserted. Today was a school-day and any adult with free time would be involved in the all-out effort for the fire victims. She and Alastair had it to themselves.

They booked in to a motel above the town. Claire's room was at the front of the building. Alastair brought her case in and left her.

'Swimming suit,' he commanded. 'I'll meet you in front in twenty minutes.'

Claire pulled the curtains and gazed in awe at the view beneath her. The sea glistened and sparkled in the morning sun. Far out she could make out a fishing boat, bobbing on the gentle swell. As far as the eye could see stretched the massive cliffs.

She stood for a few minutes, quietly soaking in the splendour before her. There was one more day left to her in this country. She knew with a cold certainty that she could never come back.

Alastair was waiting. She pulled her mind back to practicalities and crossed to her suitcase, searching for her swim-suit and sandals. Her swim-suit was not revealing, carefully chosen to hide the scars remaining high on her thigh from the accident all those years ago, but after glancing at herself in the mirror she pulled a soft Indian cotton dress over the top. She emerged to find Alastair wearing only his swimming-trunks, a towel flung loosely over his shoulders.

He was gazing out to sea, but turned and smiled at her as she approached, holding out his hand.

'Come on, Claire. It's calling us. Are those legs of yours up to the walk down to the beach?'

Claire looked down at the proffered hand, then back up to the crinkling eyes. This was her last day, and she was going to enjoy it, come what may. She placed her hand in his.

'Walk? I'm going to run!'

The day was magic. Claire blocked the thought of the following day and savoured each precious moment.

The sea was glorious. The intense heat of the past few days had faded, but it was stil too hot to be comfortable for long on the beach. Claire was in the water as soon as they reached the beach and found, to her pleasure, that Alastair was as strong a swimmer as she.

'I'll beat you to the jetty,' she called as they dived into the surf.

'Claire! Wait!' Alastair called out in alarm. The jetty was far out, at the entrance to the cove, but Claire was already gone, her lithe figure cutting a swathe through the glistening water. Alastair stood chest-deep in the surf, watching her swim away from him, then with a grin took off after her. If she could swim like that there was no need to fear for her safety.

His stroke was slower than hers, but more powerful. In a few moments he had caught her and allowed himself to slow so they were swimming side by side, stroke for stroke. Claire let herself fall half a body length behind and felt the pull of his wake. She relaxed into the rhythm of the swim, glorying in the physical power of their two bodies.

Then the jetty was before them. With a hundred metres to go Claire broke ahead. Having let him do the work for most of the way she still had power to spare. She surged forward, putting everything into the last few metres, and touched the wooden pile a split second before him. He came up behind her, laughing and gasping.

'You little wretch! You used me to pull you along.'

'What are men for if not to be used?' she asked demurely, then dived away from him as he reached to duck her. She swam and dived nimbly around the pylons. His larger frame could not manoeuvre with such speed, and he finally resorted to perching on a wooden stay and throwing up a huge splash of water at her every time she emerged above the surface.

Laughing, she deserted him on his perch and started the long swim back to the beach. She swam slowly, savouring the feel of the cool water against her skin.

As she relaxed once again into the rhythm of her stroke she became aware of Alastair. He had come easily up behind her and was now surfing easily home in her wake.

Nimbly she turned and dived under water, coming up to butt him firmly in the stomach, then twisted out of his reach. She swam fast, but over a long distance was no match for him. Once again he rode her wake, until the breaking surf showed them they were back in shallow water.

Claire found her feet, gasping and laughing, pushing the streaming strands of hair back out of her eyes. She turned to Alastair cautiously, to find him advancing with definite purpose. She drew back, but the pounding surf caught her and threw her almost against him. He did the rest. With a roar of triumph he swept her up and held her at head height.

'Put me down, you wretch!'

'Anything you say, ma'am.' With a grin he whirled her about and threw her high into an oncoming breaker.

When she finally emerged, choking and spluttering, he was already high on the beach, towelling himself dry. She followed.

'You're not a woman, you're a mermaid,' he threw at her as he tossed her a towel.

'You don't swim so badly yourself.'

'Just as well, if I'm to keep up with you,' he retorted enigmatically. He finished towelling himself and spun her round, rubbing his towel down her back. 'Sunburn cream now, my English rose, or I'll send you back to your parents looking like a broiled lobster.'

'I can put it on,' she demurred, reaching for the bottle.

He held on to it. 'Claire Bannon, this is your day for doing what you're told. My mother has laid it on me to look after you, and that's what I intend to do. Submit.'

Claire submitted. She lay on the towel in the brilliant sunshine while Alastair carefully rubbed the cream all over her. The pleasure was exquisite. She rolled on to her front to allow him to rub her back, and the deep backward and forward stroking went on and on.

'It must be coated by now,' she protested sleepily, the heat of the sun and the soft throb of the surf making everything seem very far away.

'I'll let you know when I'm through,' he replied. 'Relax.'

She slept.

When she woke he was still there, watching the gentle swell of the surf. He had rigged his towel on some driftwood to shade her healing legs and his body was shading her face. Claire lay drowsily watching him, soaking in the hard, muscled body, the eyes creased against the sun. Sensing her eyes on him, he turned to look down at her, a quizzical look on his face. She blushed, but he was already on his feet, reaching down to pull her to her feet.

'Come on—another swim before lunch.'

Afterwards they ate sandwiches from the kiosk above the beach, feeding their crusts to the squawking gulls who gathered at the first rustle of a paper bag. Claire's tensions had evaporated. Perhaps they could still part as friends. Would there be some comfort in that? She shook her head at the thought and drove it to the back of her mind. Today was for enjoyment.

The afternoon they spent sightseeing. They wandered back up to the motel, showered and changed and drove the few kilometres to see the coast's most spectacular scenery—the Twelve Apostles, giant outcrops of rock towering above the surf; London Bridge, a huge arch of rock with the waves breaking through it.

'You're not seeing it at its best,' Alastair lamented.

'But it's fantastic!' Alastair had brought her out over the narrow path crossing London Bridge's arch. She stood high above the surf, the wind streaming through her hair, glorying in the smell and sight of the sea.

He shook his head. 'Come here in winter when a storm's blowing. The cliffs are a mass of breaking foam and where we're standing now would be suicidal. If the wind didn't blow you off the spray would blind you.'

'Right up here?'

'Right up here,' he said firmly. 'I'll bring you back in July.'

'Alastair,' she said softly, a weak feeling in the pit of her stomach, 'I won't be here in July.'

He looked down at her puzzled eyes and gave her a reassuring smile. 'That's right—I forgot. Neither you will.'

It was enough to spoil her light-hearted mood and she was quiet for the rest of the afternoon. Alastair continued to be cheerful, acting, Claire thought resentfully, like a tour guide intent on giving his charge value for money. As they drove back into the motel car park she felt listless and dispirited.

'Half an hour's rest,' ordered Alastair. 'Then something casual to wear and I'll meet you back at the car.'

'But aren't we having dinner here?' Claire asked. The motel had a pleasant-looking restaurant attached. Dinner and bed and then it's over, she was thinking.

Alastair was shaking his head. 'Sorry, ma'am, dinner is booked somewhere else. I'm in charge of this trip.'

Claire emerged half an hour later wearing soft cream trousers and a loose-fitting apricot silk shirt. She wasn't quite sure what Alastair meant by 'casual', but surely this should do. His eyes, as she neared the car, told her he approved. He held the door for her. As she climbed in she saw a huge picnic hamper on the back seat.

'You really did mean casual, then?' she asked with a shy smile.

'You'll do,' he replied, sliding into the driver's seat beside her. 'Believe me, you'll do.'

'So where are we going?' Claire's tone was curt and she bit her lip.

'To Loch Ard Gorge.'

'Where?'

He grinned. 'Wait and see.'

They pulled off the road about five minutes' drive out of the town and drove over a track winding across the clifftops. A tiny group of weather-worn headstones broke the monotony of the headland. Claire looked questioningly across at Alastair.

'Victims of the sinking of the *Loch Ard*,' he said briefly. 'The *Loch Ard* was a ship which sank off here back in 1878. There were only two survivors, Tom Pearce, a young seaman, and one of the passengers, Eva Carmichael, a nineteen-year-old girl whom Tom managed to pull from the surf. They sheltered in the cave here until help finally arrived.'

Claire looked at the bleak little graveyard and shuddered.

'It's a cruel country,' she murmured, almost to herself.

'You're seeing it at its cruellest,' Alastair said slowly. 'There's certainly nowhere I'd rather live.'

'That's because it's your home,' Claire said softly.

He shook his head. 'Other places, after this, hem you in. Here. . . Well, look around.' He motioned in a sweeping gesture. 'How many other people do you see? Even at peak times, in the middle of the school holidays, you can find places where you can be by yourself, places like this that look almost the same as Tom and Eva would have seen it a hundred years ago.'

Claire didn't answer. She climbed out of the car and looked round.

'Where's their cave?' She was still thinking of the frightened couple, tossed up on this strange shore in such a dreadful way.

Alastair climbed out after her, reaching back to retrieve the picnic hamper.

'Follow the track.'

Claire walked down the little path meandering towards the cliff edge, and then stopped in amazement. The inlet was cut out of the sheer rock face. The only way down was a set of wooden steps, attached precariously to the cliff wall. They wound down, backwards and forwards, to a tiny beach at the foot. There must be two hundred steps, Claire guessed. She drew back in dismay. Her hip was recovering from the jolting she had given it three days ago. She had pushed herself hard today, but this would really be stretching it. She could get down, she thought, but could she get up?

'Fret not.' Alastair came lightly up behind her and dropped the picnic hamper. Before she realised what he intended he had swung her up in his arms and was descending the stairs.

'What on earth——?' She struggled to be free,

aghast at what he intended. 'You'll never make it up again.'

'I never thought of that,' he agreed imperturbably. 'Do you fancy living in a cave while I build up some muscles?'

'Alastair!' Her voice was a squeak of indignation. 'Put me down!'

'If you don't stop struggling I'll have to,' he warned. He stopped and looked doubtfully downward. Claire looked down too, then wished she hadn't. 'It's a bit far if you make me unsteady. Keep still, there's a love.'

She gasped, but subsided. It seemed she had no choice.

As they reached the bottom he strode over to the soft sand away from the rocks and dumped her unceremoniously.

'Stay there.'

'Where do you think I might be going?' she called after him indignantly, but he was already taking the steps two at a time to fetch their meal. Peeved, she stood up and looked around.

The cove was tiny, an inlet between the rocks with the swell of the open sea rushing in and retreating. The water was deep and glistening. Not the place for a gentle bathe, she decided. She looked back at the rock behind her. The dark entrance of a cave beckoned enticingly.

By the time Alastair returned she was deep within, hidden in the darkness. She saw him venture in, searching for her, and retreated further back into the gloom.

'Claire?'

She bit back a laugh and was silent.

'Claire Bannon.' His voice was light with amusement. 'I am about to start my meal. I have a whole lobster, avocado salad, bread rolls baked this morning at the local bakery and a bottle of wine. If you'd like to starve in your cavern you're very welcome to do so. Me, I'm going to eat.' His silhouette disappeared from the mouth of the cave.

He left Claire on a bubble of suppressed laughter, but as she stood in the dim recesses she realised the laughter was close to hysteria. This light-heartedness was a front on her part, a desperate attempt not to dissolve. On Alastair's part? He showed every appearance of a man enjoying himself, happy to see her fade out of his life. Well, why not? she thought morosely. He had Sam Cray now to share his workload. Would he still marry Rowena? The question didn't bear thinking about.

She made her way drearily back out of the cave, blinking as the light hit her eyes. Alastair was lying on a rug, the picnic spread before him. As she approached he handed her up a glass of white wine.

'Your smile has slipped,' he told her, his eyes carefully studying her face.

'The cave was creepy,' she retorted defiantly. 'I don't like dark places.'

'More fool you for going in.' His tone was unsympathetic. 'You should know better than to try and evade me, you know. I've got you nicely in my power.'

Claire drew in her breath and gazed in stunned silence at the man calmly buttering a bread roll before her.

'Here you are,' he said kindly. 'Have a plate and help yourself to some lobster before I eat the lot. You'd better keep your strength up.'

'For what?'

He grinned but ignored the question.

Claire ate very little. She toyed with the lobster and drank a little wine, but she felt as if the food would choke her. She just wanted this ordeal to end, to be on the plane and away from Australia and all it meant. She was in one of the most beautiful places in the world, she acknowledged, yet she could find it in herself to hate it. She sat mutely, staring blindly out to sea.

Alastair finished his meal and cleared up the food. Apart from casting a couple of covert glances at her face he appeared cheerfully unconcerned until she felt like slapping his face. How dared he seem so happy when she felt as if she were being torn in two?

The sun slowly set as they sat there. Finally she could stand it no longer. She stood up, brushing the sand from her trousers.

'Could we go back now?'

'Now?' He seemed surprised.

'Alastair, I can't bear this. I just want to go home.' Her voice was a whisper, choked with unhappiness.

He stood then.

'Do you really, Claire? Is that what you really want?'

'Yes.'

'Claire?'

She looked up at him mutely. His hand went into his pocket, then he held it out to her.

'Then if you're sure I guess I'd better give you my farewell gift.'

She looked down. In the half light of dusk a single solitaire diamond flashed its brilliance.

'A farewell gift?' It was all she could think of to say.

'Fare well, my love. Travel safely. Keep yourself only unto me until we meet again.'

Her eyes didn't leave his face.

'I. . . I don't understand.'

'Claire Bannon,' he reached out and placed the ring gently on the third finger of her left hand, 'I'm asking you to marry me. I'm telling you that I love you, as I've loved no other woman before and will love no other woman again. I'm saying that I don't need you to support my practice, I don't need you as a medical partner. If you want to stay involved in the medical practice, well and good, but I need you only as my wife.'

She faltered, then said stupidly, 'But I'm going home.'

'That's right,' he said, with a flash of humour. 'You have a wedding to arrange. You have a month, Claire Bannon, before I arrive to claim my own.'

'A month?'

'It can't be done in less,' Alastair said apologetically. 'It wouldn't be legal.'

Claire pulled away from him, her mind in turmoil. 'But you can't. You're going to marry Rowena MacMillan.'

'Now that,' he said firmly, 'is a singularly crazy idea. The whole district has been telling me I've been going to marry Rowena since we were children. After a while it seemed like too much effort to put them right. If you think, however, that I'm going to be happy married to a girl who puts her horses before anything else when I could have you, then you've another think coming.'

'This is ridiculous.'

'Claire?'

'Yes?'

'Shut up.'

He reached down and caught her to him. Holding her hard against him, he searched her face.

'Will you marry me, my heart? You are my woman. I can't live without you, and the pain I've been seeing in your face for the past few days tells me that you can't be impervious to me.'

Claire choked on a sob. 'Alastair, don't.' She dragged her eyes away from his face. 'You're just doing this because you're grateful to me, and I can't bear it.'

'Claire Bannon!' His voice rose to a shout. 'Of all the stupid, bloody-minded women I've ever had the misfortune to meet, will you stop being so dim-witted and acknowledge that you're loved? I love you!' His voice echoed back and forth between the cliffs. 'Now are you going to tell me that you love me, or am I going to leave you down here until you come to your senses?'

'That's not fair.'

'I know it's not. Desperate straits demand desperate measures.' He picked up the picnic basket and left her, striding forcefully up the wooden stairs. Claire watched him go, her head spinning.

She stood there, immovable, as he reached the top and disappeared over the cliff edge. Moments later he reappeared and came halfway down the steps. He sat on a step and appeared to make himself comfortable.

'Well?' His voice reverberated around and around the little cove.

'I can climb up myself!' Claire shouted defiantly.

'Not while I'm here,' he rejoined placidly. 'I'll just carry you down again.'

She gazed up at him speechlessly. His laughing eyes held her, gently mocking her impotence.

'All right,' she muttered, through gritted teeth, 'I'll marry you.'

'I can't hear you,' he called. 'You'll have to say it louder.'

She met his gaze squarely. Suddenly the fears disappeared. He held her, locked to him with his eyes, and the message they gave was unmistakable. She, Claire Bannon, was loved.

'I'll marry you.' Her voice fell off to a whisper.

Alastair shook his head. 'You'll have to do better than that.'

Claire raised her head. The sand was warm on her bare feet. Behind her the murmur of the surf rose and fell. Above her was her man.

'I'll marry you!' she yelled at the top of her voice.

And then as he started down the stairs towards her, his face reflecting the joy she felt within her, she called it again, softer, the last words disappearing as he took her into his arms and held her as if he would never let her go.

'I'll marry you.'

CHAPTER TWELVE

THE tiny churchyard was crowded. April in Yorkshire was unpredictable, but this day had turned out to be magic, a glorious spring day full of the promise of summer to come. As the bridal car approached the crowd parted, the late guests hurrying in to find their seats, the interested locals out for a look scattering to be out of the way of the bride.

The big car drew up and Claire's father assisted her out. Jill, Laura and Michelle came fluttering forward from the porch, fussing over the exquisite white gown.

Claire hardly noticed. It had been a month, an interminable month. Alastair had arrived in England late last night and had driven up this morning. A month since she had seen him.

Her father linked his arm proudly through hers. Slowly they walked through the ancient porch and stood waiting at the end of the aisle.

Dorothy was there, Claire knew, ready to spend a couple of weeks with Claire's family while Alastair and she honeymooned. There she was, seated beside Claire's mother, beaming mistily back at Claire.

Deliberately Claire gazed around the church, keeping her eyes from the dark figure at the end of the deep blue carpet. There was Auntie Lil with an extraordinary hat. All these people whom she loved so much.

They were standing. The organ blared forth its triumphant march. Claire's father nudged her arm and they started forward. Finally Claire allowed herself to look.

He was there. Claire caught her breath at the sight of him. Her whole being dissolved in a mist of love for this man. His eyes sent back their own message of his pride and love. There was nothing else she needed to know. She took her place beside him and they turned together to be made one.

DON'T MISS OUT ON HOLIDAY ROMANCE!

Four specially selected brand new novels from popular authors in an attractive easy-to-pack presentation case.

THE TIGER'S LAIR
Helen Bianchin
THE GIRL HE LEFT BEHIND
Emma Goldrick
SPELLBINDING
Charlotte Lamb
FORBIDDEN ATTRACTION
Lilian Peake

This year take your own holiday romance with you.

Look out for the special pack from 29th June, 1990 priced £5.40.

2 COMPELLING READS FOR AUGUST 1990

HONOUR BOUND – Shirley Larson £2.99

The last time Shelly Armstrong had seen Justin Corbett, she'd been a tongue tied teenager overwhelmed by his good looks and opulent lifestyle. Now she was an accomplished pilot with her own flying school, and equal to Justin in all respects but one – she was still a novice at loving.

SUMMER LIGHTNING – Sandra James £2.99

The elemental passions of *Spring Thunder* come alive again in the sequel . . .
Maggie Howard is staunchly against the resumption of logging in her small Oregon town – McBride Lumber had played too often with the lives of families there. So when Jared McBride returned determined to reopen the operation, Maggie was equally determined to block his every move – whatever the cost.

W☉RLDWIDE

Zodiac Wordsearch
Competition

How would you like a years supply of Mills & Boon Romances <u>Absolutely Free</u>?

Well, you can win them! All you have to do is complete the word puzzle below and send it into us by Dec 31st 1990. The first five correct entries picked out of the bag after this date will each win a years supply of Mills & Boon Romances (Six books every month - worth over £100!) What could be easier?

S	E	C	S	I	P	R	I	A	M	F
I	U	L	C	A	N	C	E	R	L	I
S	A	I	N	I	M	E	G	N	S	R
C	A	P	R	I	C	O	R	N	U	E
S	E	I	R	A	N	G	I	S	I	O
Z	O	D	W	A	T	E	R	B	R	I
O	G	A	H	M	A	T	O	O	A	P
D	R	R	T	O	U	N	I	R	U	R
I	I	B	R	O	R	O	M	G	Q	O
A	V	I	A	N	U	A	N	C	A	C
C	E	L	E	O	S	T	A	R	S	S

Pisces	Aries	Leo	Earth	**Please turn**
Cancer	Gemini	Virgo	Star	**over for**
Scorpio	Taurus	Fire	Sign	**entry details**
Aquarius	Libra	Water	Moon	
Capricorn	Sagittarius	Zodiac	Air	

How to enter

All the words listed overleaf, below the word puzzle, are hidden in the grid. You can can find them by reading the letters forwards, backwards, up and down, or diagonally. When you find a word, circle it, or put a line through it. After you have found all the words, the left-over letters will spell a secret message that you can read from left to right, from the top of the puzzle through to the bottom.

Don't forget to fill in your name and address in the space provided and pop this page in an envelope (you don't need a stamp) and post it today.   Competition closes Dec 31st 1990.

Only one entry per household (more than one will render the entry invalid).

Mills & Boon Competition
Freepost
P.O. Box 236
Croydon
Surrey CR9 9EL

Hidden message _____

_____

Are you a Reader Service subscriber.   Yes ❑   No ❑

Name_____

Address_____

_____

_____

_____ **Postcode**_____

You may be mailed with other offers as a result of entering this competition.
If you would prefer not to be mailed please tick the box. No ❑

COMP9